In Search of
Number Five

by

Irwinette Crite

RoseDog Books

PITTSBURGH, PENNSYLVANIA 15238

RoseDog Books
585 Alpha Drive
Pittsburgh, PA 15238
Visit our website at *www.rosedogbookstore.com*

ISBN: 978-1-4809-7256-8
eISBN: 978-1-4809-7233-9

Introduction

Getting started has been most difficult actually this is my second beginning. I have been telling people for years I was going to write my life story. I started and stopped two or three times over the years because writing and remembering causes me to relive the past and that is painful. I took so long to begin this time new problems threaten my ability to write facts. Many of the older generation, those who were there and knew the family history, are dead. Valued information and needed facts were buried with them. Not that they would have told me much anyway; this is a closed mouthed family and time. Kids were sent from the room as grownups talked. If you were not there to witness it, you were not informed. If you asked, you got crazy answers and thought of as an intruder. There is one person still alive from that era that was old enough at the time to remember some of the family history, my sister, Mary who is now eighty-two years old. The problem with that is Mary never found the need to recall events exactly as they occurred. I'm sure she cared less whether what she related really took place or not. In her mind that is the way it was. Frankly, I doubt she ever bothered to differentiate between what events were real from what she fantasized them to be. For instance, her name was Mary, but she called herself Marie. She fancied herself as Spanish. I tried asking her simple questions about my mother's illness. She hemmed and hawed so much I became leery of her answers. I discovered that her account of past events was tainted with hate and shaded at best. I am not sure the relationship shared between Mom and Mary was as wonderful as my relationship with Mom. Mary often made comments that suggest she felt unloved by everyone except Aunt Katherine. Seems she really admired Aunt Katherine. She spoke of her with a smile on her face. Then at other times Mary related her wonderful experiences as a child and teen with Mom. Knowing what Mary really felt or who she really was, was puzzling because she camouflaged herself in fantasy so much. It is as if more than one personality existed in her, one happy the other bitter.

To save myself some grief and to spare the feelings of those I love, I changed some names. In some instance, especially if I was unsure it was a fact, I took writers privilege and changed the entire setting. So reader if you trace facts some may not pan out. Bear with me. It's the way I heard it.

"Why did I write this?" a friend asked. The words keep running through my head. I felt a need to sort my thoughts by putting those words in writing.

In the summer, somewhere around 1936, there was a flood in Pennsylvania. Pittsburgh was one of the cities most devastated. Flood water was as high, in some areas, as the second story of the buildings. Basements, some bedrooms, and kitchens were flooded in low places with dirty water. Electrical power was out, food and clean water was hard to come by. Candles and coal oil lamps were being used for light. Transportation was by row boat—provided you had one or knew someone who did.

It was hot; so hot breathing in was like breathing steam. Your clothes were sticking to your wet back. It was a hot, muggy, mosquito filled summer. It had rained for thirty-plus days. The river's water had risen out of its banks. Many of the homes in this town were flooded. Life was not good. Most people had little money. Some men, in order to find work, as well as her man, were out of town working. Mom was home alone with the kids and pregnant for the tenth time.

Her legs and feet were swelling more each day. They looked tight and shiny. During the day, her feet would swell so tight she found it difficult to wear shoes. Her waist measurement had doubled and her back was beginning to sway.

Housework was tiring and climbing the stairs was an effort. Her pace had gone from a light bounce to an unattractive waddle. Her breast had grown heavy and cumbersome. They leaked, yellow sticky fluid at awkward times, spotting the front of her tops. Most of her blouses and tops had become ill-fitted and faded, especially her bras. Money was so scarce that buying clothes was not possible; replacing her worn bras was not an option. She made do with those she had; no matter the fit or color.

Mom never complained about her needs physical or emotional and tried to hide her stress from all of it, but it wore badly on her personality, and unmasked unpleasantly on her face. So much so that Mom's sisters were becoming concerned about her welfare. Mom had not acted like herself for some time. Her behavior had notable changed. She had begun doing things that gave cause for concern. It appeared she purposely pushed a window down with her daughter Mary's head. Mary was bent over with her head hanging out of a window. Mary was not badly hurt, but everyone wondered if this act was intentional or really an accident. The question was how Mom had not noticed Mary leaning out of that window.

Even more revealing than that incident was the fact that Mom had always taken pride in her appearance, particularly her beautiful red hair. Lately her hair, clothes, and general appearance seemed unkept. She was distant and preoccupied much of the time. Her eyes had always had a captive appeal, but now they had a sad and troubled gaze.

Those who noticed or cared thought, Mom just needed a rest; the pregnancy was too much. What with nine kids already to care for, another on the way and having to perform as mother and father with her husband away working much of the time. It was enough to fray anyone. There was never time for self, very little money, mounting bills, and sometimes an inadequate amount of food. Added to all of this, was the smothering feeling of being caged because of the lingering flood. There had been floods before, but this one just would not go away.

One Tuesday, around midday, Mom was summoned to the hospital. She left her school aged children at home and boarded the small boat which came for her. Eddie, Leo, and Mary the older children were out of the house working. Her husband was working in a coal mine, in a little shanty town somewhere up state. Mom was hesitant about leaving the six, smaller children alone, but the boat was small and not able to carry everyone. The children had been okay alone for short times before, she thought, and besides the hospital were not very far.

Entering the hospital must have felt good. The outing was needed. This seemed such a clean and dry place after passing through so much devastation. Clean halls that smelled of ether. It was a familiar smell in hospitals, in the thirties and forties. I guess Mom wondered what was so urgent about her care that could not wait until her next appointment. After all she felt fine. But the calm and meek person she was, always followed instruction, she came as asked. Now she sat waiting in a four by nine room. As she sat, her mind drifted to things she could be doing instead of being there.

"Mrs. Antic, I'm Doctor Blake. Your doctor was called away on an emergency and I am filling in. Your husband is John Antic?" The question in his voice caused her to feel uncomfortable.

"Yes," she said hesitantly. He nodded, eyes not moving but going up and down with his head, he begun again.

"I'm sorry to inform you your husband was in a mine accident early this morning. He was one of five men who were rushed here for care."

"How is he?" she asked.

"We tried, but we lost him about ten o'clock this morning."

Mom sat limp, paralyzed unable to move staring at the doctor trying to put the words back in his mouth. She wanted to wake up. This dream was scary. The social workers were called. When reality returned Mom was still in that little room and her husband was in fact dead. The social worker stayed to assist Mom with arrangements to have her husband's body transported to a local funeral home. All the initial arrangements had to be made at the hospital. Mom had no telephone, very little money, and possibly just enough insurance to bury him. Mom needed this help in order to understand what needed to be done next. Things were moving so fast, so sudden, so final it drained her spirit and energy.

Going home she hardly noticed, the sound of the boat paddles slapping the dirty water, the fallen trees and the mucky stench of rotting wood and small animals in the water. Time had stopped. She never noticed the setting sun, it's fiery finally its fight to redden the fading blue sky before the moon arrived. Smoke filled her nose forcing her to cough. She still sat numb. Finally, she noticed, the sky and the smoke, billowing up, black, thick and sooty. It caught her eyes, burning them. It invaded her throat and tasted bitter. She coughed and teared uncontrollably, half from the smoke but mostly from the day. While she was looking up to see where the smoke was coming from the boat was drawing closer to a wall of smoke. There, through the smoke and what appeared to be one hundred foot flames was her house radiating as if about to burst from the heat. It was her house. From the boat at a distance she heard shrill small voices, crying out helpless screams, and saw her kids running, window to window. Some jumped or fell from the caving rooms to the water through the flames. As she watched the running stopped. She fought to get out of the boat, but the men held her tight. The wall of flames rose higher and wider consuming even the water. The boat moved on. The men continued to hold her, more to comfort now, because it was done. The fire, the screams and, the caving timbers had ended. Smoke lingered leaving a red glow in the sky. Except for the resonant of Mom's heart pounding and the sound of sizzle paint frying on hot wood only quiet remained, ominous, unsettling, hanging about like an albatross, heavy and unwelcome.

Chapter One

The neighbors, those who had boats, came. Unable to help they stared solemnly, in sort of a dazed state. They looked helplessly through teary eyes, biting their bottom lip, clinching their hands in a fist until their fingernails marked their palms. They watched it all and could do nothing. There was no way anyone could have gotten through the heat of those flames to save the children. The fire had savagely engulfed the house, burning it through leaving a charred skeletal frame. The six children had either fallen through the burning floors or burned with the house. The on lookers knew there was nothing they could have done, but knowing did not help the sick feeling they had.

This neighborhood was one of those melting pot neighborhoods. Multi-racial, Hispanic, German, black, and Italian, all making ends meet getting by as best they could on what little they had. They helped each other wherever there was need. Kids in this neighborhood ate from one house to the other. While playing with the child whose parent called them to eat. If another child was there they ate, too. They spent the night at each other's home. No one thought a thing about it. This was a common practice. The six children who had just died spent a lot of time at most of these neighbors' homes. They had eaten, found comfort and slept there. These were not mere neighbors. They had been part time parent and full time friends. They just starred, dazed, clutching each other without words, needing comfort, trying to cope, with what had taken place. I'm sure they had a million thoughts, too many to make sense of. They were sad this happened, but certainly grateful it was not their immediate family to who it happened.

Aunt Katherine, Mom's sister-in-law, soon arrived, as did other family members. Everyone panicked and wanting to help, but Aunt Katherine, all four foot eight inches of her, was without a doubt in charge. Mom, unable to endure was taken home by her sister Naomi. The police and the coroner spoke at length with Aunt Katherine. They wanted all the details like why were the children home alone and how did the fire begin. These like other questions would go unanswered.

Naomi moved Mom in with her, the night of the fire. Her house was very small so she was unable to take in the older children. Consequently, they had to move in with Aunt Katherine. At this point Mom was not capable of caring for the children. She needed care herself. She needed a refuge, a quiet place with no demands and no expectations. Aunt Naomi's house was a good place for that. It offered quiet. There were no children to remind Mom of her lost. It was time for healing. Mom had been battered, pushed beyond desolation. After she barred her husband and last child, she was unable to function. She stopped talking and had to be reminded to eat. Looking at Mom anyone could see she was in pain, but no one knew what to do or how to comfort her. Days, weeks went by nothing changed. The more time passed the more dependent and remote Mom became.

Aunt Naomi was patient and gentle with Mom. Caring for Mom was not new for her. Aunt Naomi helped raise Mom as a child because Mom's mother died when she was born. Aunt Naomi was the older sister. She encouraged Mom to eat, rest, and go on with life past the pain.

The mud, the debris, and the awful smell from the flood had gone. The cleanup was well in progress. Most everyone had return to life as usual. The sky was blue the sun was out the morning Mom opened an umbrella wearing nothing and paraded down the street. It was time. More help than Aunt Naomi was capable of giving was needed. The family doctor suggested Mom be treated in Mayview Mental Hospital. The family gathered and decided their course of action for caring for the remaining children and the unborn baby. When the baby was born, since Aunt Naomi did not work and had no children staying with her, the family decided she would be the one to go get the baby after it was born and care for it until Mom recovered. Plans were made to have Mom committed and transported to Mayview Mental Hospital.

The ride to Mayview was uncomfortable lying strapped to a stretcher. The air was sticky hot, and the bedding underneath her hard and the top cover was stiff and scratchy. She remembered there was this odd little man who sat looking down at her the whole way. As he sat, he looked, but he was really was not paying attention. Occasionally he muttered, "It'll be alright." Attempting to pat her arm and read a comic book. His words lacked sincerity. They seemed more like a trained response. His actions were cold, as was this whole experience. After what seemed like an endless period of time the ambulance bumped over cobble stone and shook to a rocky stop. Two people in starched white long dressed came to help roll the gurney. Neither of them seemed to care that there was a person on the stretcher. They grabbed and jerked, turned and twisted the stretcher until her stomach was sick and she began to vomit. They stuck a cold pan under her face abruptly turned her on her side and continued to roll the stretcher through the long hall. Her face hurt with the metal pan under it. The ceilings were rusted in spots, paint chipped and cracked with lines that resembled spider legs. Molded black gray wire covered the half-light dome lights overhead. There was ugly faded white tile on the hall walls. The big windows looming high on the walls had intrusive streams of sunlight. They were mostly dirty, curtain-less, shade-less, and barred.

The stench of disinfect, mildewed mops, and urine was enough to make the strongest stomach sick. Faded, glossy white ceramic tile and mildew spotted mortar on the walls made each hallway, blah and endless. Linen carts and large mop buckets cluttered a portion of the hall. The staff was much the same as the paint blah and unfriendly.

The first days were the worst. The many medications, awful, endless treatments, questions, and more questions, unfamiliar rooms, people and food made life unbearable. As days turned into weeks which dragged on to months it was a blessing that for a long period of time Mom was not aware of time or place. Being confined; being told what to do, when to do it, what medicines to take, when to eat, where to sit, how to bath, and when to sleep seemed to have no consequence.

Mom did not remember exactly when but one day it all mattered. This seemed unwarranted punishment for a crime she could not recall committing. She became aware of the meanness of this place and wanted it to be over. She wanted to go home. Being there became frightening. It was not long before Mom knew when her treatments were due as well as what the pain felt like that went along with them. She feared she would be made insane if the shock therapy continued or the medications were not stopped.

Much of the treatment for mental illness in the early 1930s was harsh, and experimental. The treatment, as well as the providers, were anything but therapeutic and definitely not kind.

The environment was vindictive, hostile and lonely. The nurses' personalities were unsympathetic. Some of them seemed to enjoy the power giving these treatments gave them. The male attendants treated the male patients rough and touched the female patients in ways that could be avoided. Possible this behavior stemmed from lack of training or maybe it was just because they could. There were no rules about this type of behavior that anyone would argue about back then. There were even whispers of women who were frightened of the night especially if two male attendants were assigned together on a ward, some female patients were taken advantage of. Some male and even some female attendants, used their position to show dominance. Resistance to their demands was treated as a challenge to authority and warranted wrath sometimes immediate, sometimes later usually when the patient was alone or in a shower. Body beatings were common using soap wrapped in a wet wash cloth as not to leave bruises on the face. If a patient fought back by hitting or biting that patient's chart was labeled hostile. Consequently, he or she would be shuffled to an in house dentist; to have their two front teeth removed. As a rule, more medication and indeed a stronger sedative was added to their medication regime to slow them down.

Mom said she was always frightened by this place, the sounds made her fear worst. There was no sound proofing. Day and night there was always noise, screaming and chatter in the halls and from the vents.

I don't know if Mom ever gave up hope of going home, she never said. She said she just existed day to day with no expectations.

She couldn't recall, but tried to count and reckoned she must have been confined in that hell hole four years, four years of humiliation, cleansing enemas and electric shock. Four years of hurt and hurtful things. Being stripped naked and held in ice baths until her body quaked from chill. Being strapped down and having a two-inch rubber hose pushed up her rectum allowing cold water to flood in her body until it convulsed. This was the finale abdominal cramping climaxing in violent vomiting, Dehydration and days of being sick until it happened again. Then there were men who forced her down on a metal table, and affixed electrodes to her temples, having her jaws force fully opened until her face bruised and bleed. Having a bite block jammed between her teeth and electrical current applied to the electrodes until she seized, and frothed at the mouth. Imagine the embarrassment and humbling feeling of relieving her bowel and bladder on herself before passing out. Four years, four years of this torture, sometimes twice a week, in the name of treatment for a mental breakdown. Horrible, unbelievable treatments that were supposed to shock her mind back to reality. She thought at least she kept her front teeth.

Chapter Two

Who knows why Aunt Naomi decided not to come back? It may have been after caring for the baby so long and feeling like he belonged to her, she feared losing the baby. Maybe she never visited. Possible when she was told to come get Mom because she was well enough to go home. Of course Aunt Naomi was not coming back to get Mom after all how could she keep the baby. How could she explain to him that she was not really his mother, as she had told him? That his real mother was well and would soon be coming to take him home. The when of it is anybody's guess, but the why is not a mystery.

There was a talkative Euro-Asian /black man who one day it became noticeable even to Mom that this delightful postman always looked forward to talking with her. Even though no mail was delivered to her he came.

He had to have known she had no one. Mom was better and looked forward to the company. He was silly and flirty and made her laugh. Mom was quietly pretty and held his interest. She could not recall too much of the past and he never discussed much of his. This was a good match. He wondered why no family came to visit and why no one took her home on leave.

He came more often. They were allowed to walk in the gardens. It was good to have a friend. It was as if she had been asleep for four years and was rising to a new life new love, new, self and, new thoughts. When Irwin was around life was warm and not so scary. The past was gone there was no family that showed interest, no friends, no kids that visited, no anything. The slate was wiped. She remembered little of the past including people. It seemed people who had known her had also forgotten.

There was Irwin, bright and funny; she could not help but feel the love he felt for her. He always made a fuss. He told her how he loved her red hair and how pretty she was. He moved close and made a slow gesture. He touched and caressed her soft submissive skin; skin that had not been touched by a man that way in over four years. No one had made love to her, kissed her ears, or laid naked over her in a long time.

She must have had feelings that had been stored for a long time. Irwin brought rushing to the surface. She was excited by him. Her body responded to his gentle touch.

She knew there were secluded rooms in the hospital where they could be alone. She had four years to explore this building. She had used these rooms before to escape and be safe with her thoughts. This particular room was her favorite she explained. It was a quiet room away from other and larger than most rooms. She figured it must have served as a ward at one time. She had visited this space countless times alone. This was different. She could share it with Irwin. It was in a distant corner in the top floor of the building.

From the windows, she could see flickering sunlight feathering through the pines. The trees bowed and swayed, playing in the sun shading the window and feathering the light. In the back of the room was an old iron bed with a broken side -rail and a dusty unmade mattress. The bed seems to have been waiting for them, as was the serenity. In spite of all its wretchedness the room held a quaint beauty and charm.

Mom and Irwin sat kissing on the bed, touching and enjoying each other. At last having quiet time with each other; the feeling, like none other. They held each other their bodies, finally soft against one another. The anticipation turned into pleasured muffles, with no sounds other than that their bodies made. The movement of the mattress striking the head rail made a tapping sound melodied their passion. The bed coils squeaked in soft rhythmic harmony. Mom and Irwin did not hear. They were tuned only to one another caught in that place which removes all earth's latch on the here and now. In those precious hours between morning and noon, I was conceived.

From a shaded window partially opened a cool breeze touched and moved gently over their heated bodies. In the distance, they could hear the sounds of fall, wind rustling through, gently moving the evergreens, and the sound of geese trumpeting as they flew. Irwin held her firm close to his body. They laid there not talking. Words were not needed; both could feel this was a beginning.

The days and months to follow were better not because the environment improved, but because Mom had. As if she had been in a long sleep she emerged aware that there was life to live Months had passed since that special September afternoon. It was December, nearing Christmas. Snow-covered the grounds, the tree branches, and what remained of fall. Large icicles hung from the corners of the buildings and extended off the gutter and drains. Mom remembered she liked to snap them off and lick the cold. She thought the snow beautiful and enjoyed looking at it from the window; she even thought of building a snowman. She thought it might be fun to roll down the hills in it.

Irwin came that evening. His demeanor had changed. Mom had rarely seen him serious. He told Mom he had been to the administration office to ask if her family was planning to take her home soon. Since Mom was not receiving physical treatment any longer and only few medication, it seemed to him she should be released. Unfortunately, he was told there was no such plan. Her family had not shown concern, nor been to see her in three years. To him this meant Mom was never going to be released. Unless family was available to except responsible the committed patient, even though they were now well, that patient could not be discharged from Mayview Mental Hospital. Some patients were confined there so long they lived out their life and died, without ever returning to their home.

Not to burden Mom he changed the subject. Irwin helped her on with the new coat he bought her. She petted the coat and held him with adoration. They walked, out the door onto the porch and down the stairs. Irwin had already decided it was up to him to find a way to get her released so he could be with her more. He liked taking care of her. She seemed so innocent and helpless.

Days became very long for Mom now that she was alert again and with new and full understanding. She had the ability to observe what she and others were going through which made her even more she wants to be out of there. She wanted a new start, but month after month no change.

It was late in the month of February while sleeping one-night Mom was awakened by movement in her body. Her stomach was fluttering on the inside. She opened her eyes expecting pain and to be sick, but the flutter happened briefly and did not happen again. She fell back to sleep. In the morning she recalled the flutter, but so familiar with waking up vomiting from some pill she was made to take or some treatment she was relieved to be okay. As soon as Irwin came she told him about her night. Knowing the food there was not always prepared well he worried she had eaten something bad. He said, "Your stomach does look bloated a little." He asked had she not noticed it. She said yes, but did not want to say anything because she did not want any more medicine.

After Irwin left that night, she tried to remember if she had missed a period. Unless it comes this month, she thought, she was sure she had missed at least two, maybe three. Sometimes this happened as a side effect from with taking some of the medications. Then she thought, I am not taking a lot of medicines now, haven't for a while. She thought about this for a long time and sleep came.

In the morning, Mom was seen by a nurse who she told about the bloating and the missed periods. A pregnancy test was run, which quickly revealed that she was indeed pregnant. Although Mom never said with whom she had been intimate. Everyone knew Irwin was the father no one thought otherwise. It was well known he loved her. The administration notified him to come in for consultation on what to do about this situation. Irwin came as soon as work was over. When told of the circumstance and asked if he was responsible he never denied it. In fact, he smiled inside; a way had been found to get her out of that place. His prayers answered.

That evening Irwin asked Mom if she would marry him. He told her he knew about the baby and wanted them to be a family. He said he did not have much, but was willing to share what he had. I recently discovered he failed to mention he was already married. In those days, men, some men didn't get divorced they just changed cities and moved on. Mom gave the question no thought, she never paused. "Yes!" she eagerly replied. In what seemed like months, but really only a matter of weeks, papers were prepared, a blood test drawn, a license was purchased and the chaplain married them. Irwin was now her family. It took a moment for him to digest the reality of the power and significance of his position. When it all hit him he began the process of legal guardianship. In one month two days after four years of confinement, Mom walked out of Mayview Mental Hospital to go home, home with Irwin. Ironic she thought, a husband taken from her got her there. A baby stolen from her kept her there and now a husband who accepts her and a baby given her that sends her home. God is good.

Chapter Three

Moravian Way

Off East Ohio Street, the right side of a brown wood triplex, twelve steps up, second floor, door on the left, no bath, no inside toilet one bed room home a living room, and true happiness. Mom stood in the living room tears in her eyes looking at the future. Irwin gently took her hand. She turned to him and rubbed her forehead back and forward across his chest then they walked. Didn't matter it had been Irwin's apartment for a while both enjoyed looking at the rooms for the first time.

In his haste to marry and get his new bride home he had forgotten to put her on his insurance, but soon made the arrangements because their baby was to arrive in two months. There was a lot of excitement about the baby. This was Irwin's first baby. They both wanted this time to be perfect. They did not have a lot of money to spend, but enough to get a white crib, a few blankets and undershirts. Not too much could be bought because of superstition. It was bad luck to count your chickens before they hatched, as they use to say. No one bought a lot for a baby that was not born. It just wasn't done. There was always the unspoken fear of the baby dying or the momma. Momma use to say, "If I live and nothing happens," I'll do this and so. She counted each day a blessing and most of the time did not count past that day.

Irwin sang as he cleaned and cooked. He loved doing this. Mom would sit and watch him in admiration. Seemed she could not take her eyes from him when he was home and he wanted her near.

Mother's Day came he picked flowers for her. She let him feel the baby kick. They supposed it was a foot rising up in her stomach. They smiled and put their hands on it until it went away.

May 16, 1941, during lunch it was time. Irwin was at work. Mom waited until he got home, she would never go to a hospital alone again so she waited until Irwin was off. He was panicked when he arrived and saw her in so much pain he went downstairs, called a cab and they rushed eight blocks to Allegheny General Hospital, barely making it before I was born. My mother became ill during my birth and before she saw me. She said she thought she was told I was a boy so she named me Irwin. When she recovered, fourteen days later, she discovered I was a girl. She was told she had an option to rename if she desired. She promptly said, put an ET on her name. I do not believe she thought too much of what difficulty people would have pronouncing this name in the future. She wanted the name to honor Irwin and me to be a living symbol of their happiness. I'm sure she said the name to herself and liked the sound, but I do not recall her ever calling me by that name aloud. She always called me Irvie. As a result of the mix up I have two birth certificates one says I am a male the other a female both with names that are spelled wrong. Fittingly my life began with a mix up. Nevertheless, I was born.

When I knew anyone I knew my father. I loved him and I knew I was the apple of his eye. I could see it in his eyes how they lit and his smile grew when he looked at me and the joy in his face as he smiled at me. He never tried to hide the fact that he adored me. He threw me high up, he bounced me on his knee, he often took me with him; and if he was out he bought me fuzzy toys. He always had a hankie in his back pocket and pulled it free to wipe my nose or face. That I didn't like. I was afraid he had already used it. My father, my father as wonderful as he was in all his glory was a drinking man. I remember him coming up the stairs to the house shouting, "Greetings and salutations! Is everybody happy?" As he entered the door, if he made it, he would say, "Should I throw my hat in first?" He wore a large, flat, wool golfer's cap that he would toss in the door. If Mom didn't throw it back out, he'd say, "Guess it's safe to enter," and he would come in give Mom a big grandiose bow arms outstretched for her to hug him, which she always did. Then they would dance in a circle she would kiss him and they would talk. I never heard what was said, but I saw how Mom would glow and shyly smile. Then Dad would say, "I'm feeling fancy," and would strut off to bed. I loved to watch them they were so magical. They were beautiful. I thought being in love must be wonderful. I use to dream of a relationship that offered a feeling like that. One that would light my face when I heard his footsteps and seeing him would make my heart increase in beat.

My dad is the only one I have ever known who could fall up the steps and sleep there if no one pulled him in the door. My Uncle Jim or Brother Eddie, if Eddie were home on leave, would usually go out and walk him in. Then the three of them would out talk each other the rest of the night. Dad would get on the old piano stool spin around and play that piano as if he was in a speak easy. I was young but I loved it. I loved the activity and the joy in the room. The neighbors would come upstairs not to complain about the noise but to join in. They all would drink homemade brew, dance and sing out of tune. It was a happy time and they were happy people. Mom would open cans of sardines, some mustard some oil, onions, crackers, and limburger cheese and put it on the piano. That had to be the stinkiest cheese on the planet. I couldn't get past the smell let alone eat it, but Mom, Dad, and the upstairs neighbors, the Bells, loved it. This went on in the middle of the night. It was a good time no thought about the mounting bills, low pay it was a fun time with no worries.

Dad frequented the neighborhood pubs, everybody there knew him. On some weekends he took me with him, much to my mother's disapproval, but dad was the last word and being the head of his house always had the final say and about me there was no argument. I was his daughter his pride and joy. Out of respect and unbelievable love for him Mom always bowed to his wishes. I always thought when I grow up I won't let anyone run me as he does her though she never seemed to mind. Dad could be sitting on the salt shaker and he'd say, "Cleo, where's the salt?" and Mom could be across the room and would almost run to hand the shaker to him. I thought this very strange. As a child I did not understand the reason for this behavior. As I grew I did. It is called love and respect. Mom never ate before serving my dad and stood ready to carry out his every wish at any time.

Dad had a heavy wool overcoat. I remember he would carry me close to his shoulder and sometime depending on the weather he would wrap me inside the coat with him. I would always be warm. When we arrived at the pub he would sit me on the end of the bar. From there I could look down and see the large brass rails around the bottom of the bar. I was fascinated by it. The rail was so shiny. I remember peeping over almost falling to be able to see the large gold spittoons at each corner of the room and on the floor near the bowed rail. I liked the pub it was fun. I just loved the liveliness, the crowd, the laughter, the smell of the beer and especially the music. During the course of the evening the ladies in the pub would hand me one to the other around the room feeding me pickled pig's feet, pork skins, and squirt pop. I suppose after two-three hours and a few too many drinks, Dad would either forget I was with him or figure he was too drunk to carry me and would stagger home alone. My mother, I'm sure would expect he would do this always knew where to find me and came quickly to retrieve me. In the mean time I sat on the corner of the bar waiting near the pistachio nut machine with a pocket full of pennies, one or two from all who passed by and saw me using the machine. I ate pistachio nuts until my fingers mouth and teeth were red from the dye on the shells. I was never feeling alone or scared. The usual crowd were always there they knew I was Irwin's little girl and everyone looked after me. Some would carry me to the juke box and let me pick a song. All were kind. Now that I look back on it I was probably safer there waiting sitting on the bar than in my dad's arms after he had been drinking. He never admitted it, but I honestly believe he knew that, and intentionally left me for Mom to retrieve. Times were different back then the neighborhood cared for the child.

My father and I were pals he would never put me in harm's way. The only thing he did which I hated was he would pull out a big white handkerchief from his pocket, wadded up, so I wondered if it had been used and wipe my nose with it. Oh, that was so terrible. I imagined his snot all over it. Then I remember shopping with Mom one day and she would not buy me a toy dog. It was a wiener dog. With long leather like ears and brown spots. The legs made a wake, wake, noise as it was pulled along. I wanted that toy so much, but either Mom could not afford it or she did not think it practical so we went home without it. It was pouring rain and dark when my Dad got home from work. I told him about the dog. He straight way went in his pocket handed Mom the money and said, "Take Bunky." Dad called me that to get the dog. Mom bundled me up and out we went into the rain to the five and ten cent store to get the dog. When Mom and I got home the finish on the dog had gotten sticky from the rain. I remember the dog was sticking to my hands. I licked my fingers they tasted salty. No matter the dog's finish was ruined I was happy. Wet toy and all it was wonderful. I still feel the joy of that moment when I remember that night. I had to be three or four years old don't remember. I just know it has been a loving lifelong memory for me.

An even greater memory to this day is the feeling that I was loved by two parents who agreed I was important. I could feel the love like a warm soft blanket. That was a good time.

My dad was so special to me he and I would sometimes sit on the back porch and eat raw shrimp dipped in hot water boiling on a hotplate, dragged through rock salt and poured with soy sauce. I learned to shell and devein a shrimp as smoothly as he. My father was a serious man he did most things he attempted well. He liked to clean. He cleaned with a passion. Mom and I knew he was not allowing, but not saying do not come in, the room where he was working so we looked in, but stayed out of that room. I could hear him singing the entire time he worked. Many nights he worked on into the early morning polishing silver, mopping and waxing the floors. He took pride in his home and his work.

Things took a strange turn it seems one day there were Mom and Dad and me at home then there were more. When did the house fill with people? My sister Mary, who was never there because she traveled a lot, came home and married Ralph, a construction worker. They moved in. My brother Leo who use to came by often, now he was moved in. Eddie my older brother was in the army, but when on leave he stayed there. Funny as crowded as it must have been everyone got along. Uncle Jim, Mom's brother would come over on Friday or Saturday night, always drunk. It was like a party there was always laughing and singing. Dad wore a flat large cap on the side of his head played on an old piano and sang and Mom and Mary would dance They played cards drank liquor, ate sardines, crackers, and Limburger cheese all night.

I loved Eddie. When he was away he wrote interesting letters at first about CC camp, but later more about Guam. It seems strange to me that still l remembers the letters because of my young age, but I do. Eddie always took the time to write me. He teased and asked if I wanted him to bring me a monkey. I was too young to know Eddie was in harm's way. Eddie was always fun. I did want that monkey though. Looking back, I didn't realize he wasn't serious, but at that age and time I took him serious. I was so excited. When I was sad took comfort in the day when Eddie would come home with my monkey.

Ralph was my second dad. I had infantile paralysis, known now as polio. I don't know when I got it or the date it went away. I do remember when it did. I just know I was unable to walk. Mom carried me or rolled me around in a large baby buggy. Ralph always got up early to prepare for work. He ate a lot and looked like a lumber jack. Ralph was a tall, very big man. He would come get me from my crib, early in the morning, wash my face, and wrap a towel around me so he and I could eat breakfast. We usually ate Franco-American spaghetti and kielbasa sausage, covered in Louisiana hot sauce. I looked forward to this every morning. After we ate he put me quietly back in the crib. He'd put his finger over his lips and say shoo, wink, and leave for work. Mom in the bed near me never moved an eyelid. When it was light Mom would get up, not knowing I had already eaten she fixed me oatmeal and pancakes and fruit and wondered why I wasn't hungry. I'll bet she worried I would waste away. I never said a word. This was my and Ralph's secret. Mom and Mary would have flipped if they knew Ralph fed me hot sauce and polish sausage for breakfast at three-thirty in the morning.

I loved Ralph. To this day I prefer last night's left over's to this morning's breakfast. I feel safer in the arms of a big man with little but a big smile then a regular guy with much to offer. My father was a man of small stature, but he was so kind, so loving in heart that I count him giant even more than big. I never thought about it before, but it's fair to say both my Dad and Ralph were dad, only different. I fault both of them though, for giving me the impression that all men were good, kind, loving as they and would treat me with love. As life happened I found that was not true.

Time passed, our house remained happy, the war got worst. I don't remember much about the time during the war. I do remember the nights when a man with a pole long enough to reach our second floor apartment window would tap on the glass yelling lights out. Mom would quickly pull the drapes shut to block the light from showing. She always looked frightened when this happened. I remember some foods were rationed. Money was not used for certain things. We shopped with black and red tokens at the A&P. The tokens felt rough and sort of looked like bingo chits. As ugly as they were those tokens were, beautiful. They allowed Mom to buy soft bread, oleo, coffee and best of all cheese. The sales clerks at the A&P all liked me and would come get me while Mom shopped. They gave me little slivers of all kinds of cheese. I always liked the cheese wrapped in the red cloth. On the way home Mom put the groceries in the buggy with me which proved to be a mistake for the bread. By the time Mom and I reached home I had stuck my hand in the center of the loaf balled it up and eaten it like dough. Yum! Now that I think about it Mom must have known what I would do to the bread because she kept putting it in the buggy with me. Wise women, she got me to eat bread.

Time passed, the war ended. Eddie came home, got married. and moved to Sharpsburg. One would think these events would have little to do with me, but not only did they but spurred major change in my life with Eddie married the house changed, My uncle Jim, Leo , and Mary worked at night for Federal Enamel. One night Mary came home early she had an accident and cut off the tip of her middle finger. Sometime later this gave her the bank roll I guess she needed to leave Ralph.

For a time, the card playing was stopped, but the drinking didn't. When the family did get together they were still loud, they would play cards, brag, and drink all night. One evening they were all in the kitchen loud as usual. I could smell the onions and Limburger cheese two rooms away. As usual I was in my chair in the bedroom. I wanted to be in the kitchen too. I made up my mind I was tired of being left out. I slid from my chair to the floor. Pulling myself weakly using my arms and hands and legs pulled me to the door in the bedroom and through the next room finally from the floor I could see in the kitchen. Those who were sober enough to notice looked stunned to see me sitting there. They must have wondered who put me there everyone knew I couldn't walk. It didn't take long though; after all that effort I was put back in my chair, tucked in my blankets and assured I was secure again. Nevertheless, I did it. I got out of my chair and I actually moved across the floor. What a moment.

Things unraveled pretty quickly after that night or so it seemed. Mom and Dad began to argue a lot. I don't know the reason, or about what I just felt helpless, isolated from one parent or the other at the time, frightened and my body felt heavy. Until this day when I hear anyone argue or are in an argument my body reacts the same. I just want the words to stop. Even though I could walk a little I was in my chair and Mom was in her bed with pneumonia. It was late in the day that summer dad came in with a striped tan suitcase in hand, a large brown cigar with a gray ash about so long on the tip. He opened the suitcase and quickly put clothes in it. He glanced around the room, folded the case close, strapped it up, then came over to my chair to kiss me. Ashes fell on my blanket. The nap sparked a little; he brushed it away, the smoke from the cigar made it hard for me to breath. The smell was unsettling, so uncomfortable; I began to coughed chocking, in my heart as well as in my lungs. Years have passed yet, even now the smell from the cigar lingers, and at odd times I smell it as clear now as then.

The pneumonia passed and Mom got well and on her feet again, but her spirit never rose. Losing my dad was something from which she and maybe I never recovered. As if someone shut sound and the worlds light off much changed about Mom and for me the day Dad walked out.

As life does, life went on; Mom got a job cleaning a doctor's office, probable so I could receive free medical care. Food kept coming, I went to school never missed a day. Mom took me there in my buggy and carried me into class. *I loved school.* It was a place where I was the same as everyone else difference only I could not go outside for recess. I was stuck in my chair. I made the best of it I ate the Jordan almonds Mom bought me and I practiced writing making my letters better.

Slowly things at home began to change. I could walk a little. Eddie was married and not in the house a lot. Leo disappeared, Ralph was not there and Mary was traveling again. Mom and I were doing okay, but the house was noticeable sad. Even at my age I knew this was not the best of times. I sensed the situation was not good, but I did not begin to imagine how bad it really was. I did not know Mom was single. I was not aware at the time my father had two wives Mom being the second making her marriage null and void. I had no idea Mom even dated anyone and now she was married. I thought when did this happen? When did Mom decide to marry, she's married to my dad, and who is this strange looking man. I had no idea he existed. I never met him. When did she date him and how long? Where did he hide until we were at the wedding reception in the very crowded front room of his house? I'd never seen him before. It was done; done Mom was married to a very black, tall gaunt scary looking man who had all the physical features of satin minus the pitchfork. His skin had no light in it black, but as it turned out not as dark as his soul or lack thereof. His eyes were sunken and he reminded me of a skeleton with skin on it and he coughed and spit a lot. Mom looked nice as she walked through the crowd wearing a gray satin, fishtail dress greeting people with a smile she must have put on with her makeup. I was walking by then so I trailed her through the room when I felt something in my eye, a cigarette ash or something. All the people seemed to be smoking. Someone seeing me wipe my eye picked me up and tried to help me. Mom turned, saw me crying and came. After that all I remember is sitting on Mom's lap on a makeup bench very scared, very unsure of what was to come. Mom married, my dad gone, my life changed. It was years later when I found out Dad was already married when he married Mom so technically they were not married. It happened a lot back then men did not divorce they just moved to another state and got lost while waiting on the first wife to die or find someone else. Who had money for a divorce?

Sharpsburg

This awful place was our new home. I didn't remember moving furniture, our clothes or having any say in the process, but here we were living in a windowless dark, filthy shotgun house, bedroom to kitchen shabby. On entry there was a linoleum floor on it was a brown smooth finished coal stove in the front room on the left. There were two baskets of coal behind the stove. Mom's bed was on the right behind the headboard was a bench in front of a vanity then a wall. There were two other bedrooms with beds on both sides of a narrow aisle. In the first bedroom room there was a cot on the left over a cellar door and a regular bed on the right with quilts on them. The cot on the right was mine, I guess I was lucky at least I had my own bed. Maybe that began the hate, maybe I took one of their beds. Lonnie's daughters Annie and Susie or Mae as her dad called her, slept together. Maybe that began the hate, I probably I took one of their beds. Thomas and Jimmy two older boys slept in the second room, one in each bed one left and one right of the aisle. They had no resemblance of brothers and it was for sure these two seriously disliked each other. They argued and even fought at every opportunity more frequently if they were in a room together over ten minutes. After being there awhile it became evident Lonnie liked the lighter kids best the treatment made the distinction clear. One step down and there was a kitchen. In it another coal stove to cook on and a small room with a toilet in it on the left. Outside a nosy screen door, a small grassless, dusty yard with a large poorly kept collie dog they kept chained to a tree and a large homemade smelly dog house. Mom and I did not have a lot, but I didn't know that people lived like this. I'm sure Mom did not see this before she moved us here.

Mom got a day jobs in Aspinwall, an exclusive residential town, just above Sharpsburg. Mom was hired to clean house and ironing for Mrs. Preston and Mrs. Blasdale Monday, Wednesday and Friday for Ms. Blasdale and Tuesday and Thursday for Ms. Preston. Mom worked hard for very little. When I was out of school I went to work with her. It was peaceful there. The homes were so pretty. I learned to cook, set a dais and play canasta. I loved to listen to Mr. Preston play the banjo. I don't know what it was about the banjo, but the sound of it stopped me in my tracks. Even now the ring of it has a particular effect on me. One I cannot explain.

Mom cooked and we served the Thanksgiving and Christmas dinner. There was so much food. The decorations were so pretty. The table always had white linen clothes on it that hung to the floor. Sometimes tall candles were placed in the center. The house, the grounds, as well as the table were always decorated for every holiday. For me the best part of the day though was after Mom and I finished serving dinner. After the guest were finished eating and had gone from the room. When the table was cleared and just the sound of the music and muffled chatter seeped into the room, Mom and I would go back into the kitchen and eat together. That's a memory I cherish, I cherish…all by itself, no gifts; it was my holiday.

I made one friend her name was Francine. She and her family lived in Aspinwall. They were live in maid and butler to a family there. Francine was able to live there, but had to attend a school in Sharpsburgh. No colored kids could attend school in Aspinwall. Yeah, this was the north with silent prejudice. While she waited for her father, who was sometimes late, picking her up after school she and I played. We danced to our choreographed routines. On Fridays I would go home with her every chance I got. I stayed until Sunday because I had to return to go to church with Mom. I loved being with that family. Francine hated it, but I never minded being told to go to bed, or eat your food. I wanted a family. As far as I was concerned she had it all. There was a mom and a dad. Not that Mom wasn't my family because she was everything to me, but I wanted my whole family again.

I wasn't jealous, I envied Francine. She had it all, always had crisp, pretty dresses, long black smooth braids with bright ribbons on them. Her house was clean and she had her own room, had two parents who seemed to love each other and her. I wanted this. I thought if I had two parents we could live like this in a clean happy house. On the weekends If not at Francine's home I was in church all day sometimes a movie in the evening. This was rare Saturday was mostly the movie day.

I liked church. I sang in the choir and I had a boyfriend there named Peter. He was the minister's son. He and I could talk and sneak to hold hands. There wasn't much time for that though there was Sunday school, singing in the choir eating lunch at the church and then evening service. On Sunday church was all day people watching everywhere and come Monday he was gone. His family must have lived in another town I don't know. Only saw Peter on Sundays. Church was a great outlet for me and Mom. It sure helped me get through the coming week.

The years I had to be in the Graham house were indescribable awful. I try, but cannot recall even one pleasant day or night there. Not a holiday, birthday or any day. While I was in bed during the early morning my step father would intentionally walk through the room where I slept so close to my bed that his hand drug slowly left and right down over me, chest to toes. He tried to touch my butt I soon learned to sleep on my side, knees to my chest, with my head covered up tightly. On regular days, Mom would leave for work before I left for school. I dressed as fast as I could to get ready to get out of there. As soon as the school yard opened, I was there. Most mornings before I left, I had to hear Lonnie spelling to Mae, "Go get Pig." Pig was some women he slept with during the day while Mom was at work. I don't think I ever saw her because I was in school when she showed up and she was gone by the afternoon. Lonnie worked at the steel mill got to the house around 6:00 A.M. and left for work around 3:00 P.M. So I heard her name being spelled a lot. She must have slept with him all day and made it out of the house by the time Mom made it there. Don't guess he knew or cared that I could spell.

One night I came in about 6:00 P.M., after dark, and opened the front door and saw Lonnie sitting straddle across Mom's chest cursing and punching her in the face. Every day of my life, every day not minus one since, this occurred does this not play over and over again and again. I get the same rage. the same hate even when I think of it as I did then. I must have been six or seven at the time. On that night, I decided to kill Lonnie. He was safe tonight only because I wasn't very strong. It had only been a short while since I had begun to walk after having polio and not walking seven years. My muscles were still weak. One evening, while we still lived on Maraven Way, it was almost dark, sky red and beautiful my brother, Eddie, Mary and Mom were in the kitchen and the usual loud laughing was going on. I wanted to be in there with the fun. No one came to get me when I yelled. Well, my head said go in there. I scooted off my chair on my blankets to the floor and with my upper body and pulling with my arms I pulled myself to the kitchen two rooms away. Everyone just stared at me. Guess they thought if I could do that I could walk so from that night on everyone grabbed me under my shoulder and walked me to and from. My feet had not learned to walk or my legs to stand but some-how with no physical therapy and God's help I got stronger and I did walk. But now clearly I needed strength. I was told Lonnie hit one of his daughters who now was locked up in some mental institution with a brass poker iron causing brain damage. It was rumored he only mar-ried Mom so she would save him the cost of his daughter's institu-tional care. Rumor was if he had a wife to care for the child she could come home. Mom must have refused the responsibility or been found incapable given her past history. Lonnie stopped pretending to love Mom even when he was sober. I don't believe he ever loved Mom. It was all for his advantage and when his plan failed he regretted the marriage. He was extremely ugly and mean to Mom. Kids are not said to understand grown up affairs but I did. I don't remember being a child. I always thought things out, planned and searched for truth.

That very same copper handled poker iron Lonnie hit his daugh-ter with was still in the coal basket behind the stove in the front room. I planned to use it. At first I only felt of its head. It gold colored, heavy and had a smooth but dented surface. Every chance I got I would go outside and find a large lump of coal from the cellar and practiced swinging at it. This built my arm muscles and my strength improved.

I wanted to be certain one swing; just one would be all I needed to crush his skull. He was thin it shouldn't take much I thought. It would be at night while he laid in a drunken sleep. I did not want any noise so no one else would wake up. But God knew, he heard my thoughts and saved me. God let me get stronger, and my legs stood firm, my arm solid, my stance perfect, but he never let me work my plan. In the seven years after that decision and I suffered there I never saw Lonnie asleep. Never saw him nap ever. Many times I thought he was asleep I would stand near the coal basket hand on the poker iron, but he would come to a full sitting position from a bent head down on his knees position in his chair by the stove and catch me staring at him. There we were eyes looking at each other a long time. In seven years he and I never exchanged one word. He had to know. It should have been clear I never hid the hate. When one of us blinked he would either call out, "Mae, bring me some bicarbonate or Jimmy, chunk these coals and put some coal in this stove." I would think another day, another day. Contrary to, that just a few blocks away, Eddie, my brother, and his wife China were two of the happiest people I have ever known lived in a place we called up the house. I spent much of my awake time there. They already had two kids, a boy and girl, two healthy children. Ruth's doctor explained to them they were not to have any more children because Ruth was not healthy, but Eddie and Ruth as we called her paid no attention to the warning. They played cards every evening and drank after the kids were asleep. Perhaps it was unintended and just one of those beautiful times, but soon Ruth was pregnant again. When the third child was being born Ruth had a long complicated delivery. This over all was well, things were back to normal, but Ruth was told not to have more children. Gloria Jean baby number three was healthy and life was good. In the night while they were asleep two months later Gloria

Jean died. She was discovered dead in her crib. The death was ruled crib death. Ruth and Eddie were destroyed they loved each other and really loved those babies.

The house that was my refuge because there was so much happiness in it. Maybe they forgot what the doctor' told them maybe they gambled, because nine months later again Ruth was pregnant once more. The pregnancy went well. Ruth had a little boy. The baby was healthy, but Ruth died on the delivery table. This turned the page for Eddie. He didn't want the baby. He was so broken he could not function. I don't think he cared he had other children.

Someone called my sister Mary back from who knows where to care for the children, but she didn't get there fast enough. Eddie was drinking heavily and behaving suicidal. He jumped from a bridge and broke both legs. Still he wanted nothing to do with his baby blaming the baby for his wife's death. This was not true, of course, still Eddie would not bring the baby home from the hospital. I'm not sure how it happened or who asked her, but Mentor, Uncle Jim's girlfriend, went to the hospital and picked up Johnny, the baby. The name Johnny is always the second born male's name in our family, so naming him was easy. All the firstborn men in the Strothers' family were named James. Now we only had two James left my nephew and my brother, Eddie James Edward. My Uncle Jim was the eldest. Unfortunately, Uncle Jim on the way to Mentor's, his girlfriend's house, sometimes drunk, would stop on a grassy shady, secluded unused end of the railroad track that halved the town to take a nap. Don't know, but I'm told one afternoon he was drunk as usual, laid on the grass covered track and went to sleep. That day a train did use that track and Uncle Jim was killed. Since that time the story has changed and the family now believe he was murdered pushed over the train treacle. The family in Sharpsburgh reached out to the girlfriend, but she was a quiet woman and did not respond.

The older two children came to live in the Graham house. My niece Janice was light skinned, Butch had a dark complexion. Right

away I saw the distinction Lonnie made in them. Lonnie as dark complected as he was, did not like anyone who was dark, not even his own
children. He and Susie did not hide their feelings. They were blatantly
cruel. They cherished Janice but Butch was demonized from the start.

Maybe insecurity on their part but knowing them as I do they
were just mean. Butch peed the bed every night. One morning
Tommy, Jimmy and I were standing in the kitchen around the cook
stove while Susie was making a sunny side up egg for her dad Lonnie.
All of a sudden Tommy hawked and spit in the eggs. It sizzled around
then crusted around the egg's edge looking like brown lace. Susie got
a spatula and carefully put the eggs on a plate without breaking the
yolk, added two strips of bacon and a biscuit and took it to her father.
When she finished serving the eggs she turned to Butch who had just
gotten up and was, moving toward the stove trying to get warm. As
soon as Susie saw him she sent him away saying he stunk. Butch, head
down looking as if he was going to cry ran into the bathroom. Bath
water had to be heated but no one moved to heat it for him. He
washed up in cold water Janice helped him put on dry clothes. As soon
as Butch came out of the bathroom Susie handed him a bottle and
told him to pea in it. After he peed in the bottle she dragged him to
the screen door in the kitchen, slapping over the face and head, beating and cursing him all the way for wetting the bed. I ran along with
him. I watched him shivering at the back door. He was so little and
so scared. I argued with Susie telling her this was wrong, but she paid
me no mind. Then the unbelievable occurred. I watched as Susie
made Butch drink his pea every drop until it was gone. This was the
first of many such mornings. Every day, every morning if Butch wet
the bed Susie made him drink his own pea. Butch was a very brave
little boy, not once did any of the older kids move to stop Susie or
help Butch. Janice and I were too small and the others too ingrained
too mean and animal like. They found this entertaining. Each time
and, day by day Butch grew more resilient. Me, I grew more hate.
Butch learned not to cry and to forgive. I learned not to cry.

One day I came in from school and the kids were gone. Mary had finely gotten there. She and her son, my nephew Jr had come and gotten them. I'm told there was a disagreement about who had the right to take the kids, but the kids left with Mary. It was wonderful. If Eddie didn't come Mary was the next best thing. I turned in the doorway and headed straight for the house the closer I got the warmer I felt. When I got there from outside I could hear the laughter the House was filled with it. It was like a warm day after a week of ice and snow. It felt good.

Mary also got the baby from Mentore; all the kids were together again, but in the coming weeks Mentors became very depressed having Johnny so long she got too close and began to feel like he was hers. Losing Johnny dealt her a big blow. This was sad but the kids needed to be together and in their home. Eddie began to father again and even stranger then that he began to visit Mentore and take Johnny so she could see him. At first he visited once in a while. Then more frequently. Eddie never said neither did Mentore that they were dating but we put two and two together. It had been hard for Eddie but he seemed to be getting through it. For as long as I remember he never stopped loving Ruth but he survived.

David, Mary's boyfriend, arrived in Sharpsburgh. I'll never forget the gleam in his eyes as he looked at Mary. I think it was so special. I wanted someone someday to look at me like that. Those at the house hoped David being there might make Mary want to stay. Things were so much better with her there. She brought life back to that house and returned to a home.

I hated everything and everyone in the Graham house and especially living there; so one day I packed very little and moved up the house. When Mom got off the street car I was there. I tried to explain why I moved to Mom without telling her the whole story. I figured she had enough to worry about and didn't need to get angry over her trifling husband trying to molest her child. As I expected my moving made Mom sad. I'm sure she thought it was her fault because I never told her about all the dodging and staying away from the house I had to do to keep from being molested. There was so much I never told. I never told Mom about Pig, the women her husband was sending for as soon as she was out the door for work. I only hoped Lonnie Graham would hurry up and die, get hit with a truck, fall from a building or get crushed in the steel mill.

The kids were out of that house safe and happy now and so was I. The house was once again complete we were all there, except for Ruth.

Living there was good. I only remember one strange instance that happened with Mary anther friend Dave. He punched her one night blacking her eye. Days went by Mary and Dave went out, guess Dave thought Mary had gotten over it. Mary smiled and seemed to forgive him. They went out Dave got drunk. Mary helped him to get home and undress. Then Mary went outside cut down the clothes line, tied Dave face down to the bed took his belt buckle and beat him raw then poured a box of salt in the wounds, He was screaming so loud a neighbor called the police.

Mary was arrested, went quietly, and spent two weeks and six days in a psychiatric unit playing crazy to avoid jail. Dave was waiting when she returned nicer than ever. After that I don't recall Mary and Dave ever having a big fight and rarely even an argument again. If nothing else, there was never a dull moment with those two. One thing I remember is the way he looked at her it was always like he was seeing her for the first time. I loved them both. Sometimes in life, but only rarely in my life, there are good periods. There are some phases I wish to remember, some I try to forget. This was one of those I want to remember.

I was about twelve years old the day I was asked to come to the office at my school. I was moved to a small room where a social worker was sitting smiling at me. In the first place I never trust strangers who smile at me. Secondly she was asking all kind of questions about my mom, her husband and where I lived and what went on there. Shortly after that I was in court in front of a judge. I should back up. Prior to that in walks my dad, who, I had not seen in maybe five years asking me where I wanted to live, with him or Mom. I missed him so much but wondered where he had been while I ducked my step father to escape being raped. Where did he **live** when I had to move in that hell hole and why did my whole life have to suffer because he left us? I still remembered the good times and loved him, but things had changed. I felt betrayed abandoned and so hurt. Nothing was decided that day I could not answer. I gathered the problem was where I was living. I was living with my sister, away from my mom so my father wanted custody. I didn't want to go back to living in that house again but during the coming days I could see the possibility of losing me to my dad was wearing on my mother. Not that I would have ever answer any differently, but this situation frightened me too. I had to choose sides. I hated that. But when asked again where I wanted to live I emphatically said, "With my Mom." I never saw my father again.

The judge with little understanding was not kind. My mother was ordered to have me move back with her in thirty days. I never told anyone, not even my mom, and I dared not tell the judge, the reason I needed to move with my sister. I'm sure that if the judge knew that in order to keep from being raped or molested by my stepfather I had to avoid being alone with or even in a room with him he would have not sent me back there. I never told Mary either because she would have killed him or gone to jail. Who would this have helped? The kids needed her.

Moving back made me sick inside. Sick, and frightened or not I have always tried to do what needed to be done, so I stored my feelings, packed my few possessions and in one hour to the courts delight I was back on the cot over the cellar door a target for rape. Another lesson: sleep very lightly.

My mom had a thirteenth birthday party for me at my Aunt Katherine's house my cousins who lived in the area were there. I remember my cousin Naomi made a wonderful cake it had green, pink, and blue layers. That was the most wonderful cake. While eating it I realized Mom and I did not really have a home. We had the church for Sunday dinner The Preston's and Bladale's for holidays and Aunt Katherine's for parties. We lived in a space behind her dresser in the front room of the Gram house. I thought about it all night. I always met Mom at the streetcar stop to say hi and help carry any bags she had. Today was different. I had a shopping bag with some things for Mom and me.

As Mom began to get off the streetcar I pushed her back on and I got on, too.

She said, "What's the problem, Revie?"

I said, "We are leaving. I don't care if we live on the street we are not going back there." The streetcar kept going Mom was looking at me but she and I sat quiet as we rode on our way to a new life.

We got off in Lawrenceville, a small stretch from down town. I remember Mom and I going from place to place to find a place to sleep. We found a rooming house and that night we slept in a rented room in a rooming house. The next day, which was Saturday, we went to Aunt Naomi's apartment building in the same area and got two rooms there.

We had a couch that pulled out, which was Mom's bed, and I slept on a rollaway. There was a two eyed bunion burner type stove in a small area which we called the kitchen. Above this little area where we cooked there was a window, outside of it there was a fire escape. Many nights I sat out there. It was like my living room. I sat out there dreaming, planning my future, and looking at the stars. I had plenty of time. There was only one other child in this apartment complex named Patty. She and I became friends, but I saw her for only short periods like Saturday and Sunday mostly. I can't remember why. Mary my sister also lived four blocks away, so I often walked to her apartment.

I made friends at my new school. I learned to dance and I was on the swim dance team and the volleyball team. Hated soft ball and loved volley ball. I was the captain of the volleyball team all four feet, eleven inches, seventy pounds of me. I had a mean spike but I had a team member a girl named Barbra Slaughter on the team would yell Slaughter when she served. When she hit that ball it moved like a weapon. The speed of that ball could have taken off your head if you got in the way of that serve. We had a great team. I liked school, I was comfortable there.

Mom and I had very little money, but after what we had been through all things considered life was better. Mom and I had many happy days just her and I. We also had our share of bad days. I remember Mom being sick in bed unable to work and us running out of food. I walked the streets one night looking for pop bottles to cash in for the three cent deposit so I could buy hamburger and baked beans. Mom called this mixture Slumgolian we both loved it. It took me most of the evening to collect enough pop bottles to cash in, but by 8:00 P.M., I had enough to buy supper. As Mom got better it really began to sink in who provided for me and what it took just to buy food. It was clear who I could depend to take care of me. It was also very clear Mom braved a lot to provide for us. Earning just five dollars a day from ironing in basements of nice homes, cleaning houses and serving food she did wonders. I can't put into words how grateful I am and what values I learned from watching Mom take life on. I still marvel when I think of the concurring spirit and calmness with which she did it.

There was an upside. Although they paid Mom poorly they provided me which quite a bit of my clothes and cosmetic. They gave Mom very nice, hand me downs. My first tube of lipstick and a large bottle of Faberge' perfume came from a trash can someone at Mom's job threw away or put it in the wastebasket so Mom would find it. Putting the things, they wanted Mom to have in the trash can seemed to be a common way of giving Mom cosmetics or delicate things by putting them in the bathroom trash basket. At first Mom would ask are you sure you don't want this, but it seemed to make them mad, so she stopped and just brought the stuff home. Because of this I dressed just as good as the other kids in my class in fact I sometimes looked better and more exclusive. The hand-me-downs were all from very upscale stores. To this day I prefer the sale rack of an exclusive store or resale boutique to a regular priced item from a regular store.

After dinner one night while I was sitting on the fire escape I saw a familiar figure ringing the entry door bell. I crawled over to see if it was who I thought. It was him, Lonnie Graham. I can't tell you the fear I felt because there were so many thoughts at once, all bad.

I stood up, held the rail, and yelled down to him to go away.

He said, "Get your mother."

I said, "Go away or I'll throw lye and night water on you."

He kept ringing the bell. I was afraid someone in the apartments would get tired of hearing the ringing and banging on the door and just open the door. I crawled back in the window found the chamber pot we used at night to avoid going out in the hall in our night clothes to the common bathroom. It was not full but had smelly disinfectant in it and some pea. I added the hottest water I could find boiling in the teapot and climbed back out the window. Mom was asleep tired from the day at work. I threw the pea, toilet paper and hot water on him. He tried to duck, but some got him. He ran very quickly back to his car.

The next time I heard about him it was good news a year or two later. One of Lonnie's kids sent word he had died. Stomach cancer, I believe. A fitting end. I told Mom. Mom, being the kind and forgiving spirit she was for a reason I yet fail to understand, wanted to attend his funeral. I agreed we would go only if I could take a record player, playing, "I'm glad you're gone, you rascal, you," loudly in the front row and I could wear a red dress and put ashes in his coffin. We did not attend. I hope they buried his body face down facing hell where he belonged. I'm sure he went there and put satin on the shelf and took over.

The only thing this reptile–all due respect to reptiles—did right was work, which afforded Mom a decent widow's social security check. What a blessing that was. Mom earned every dime of it. Did I ever tell Mom he came to talk to her, before he died? Absolutely not. I devoted my life as long as she lived protecting her and trying to give her happy moments. So no I never told her that organism showed up. Whatever he did or said to get her to marry him, in the first place, he may have tried again. It may have made her go back with him because Mom was very kind and forgiving. I am, too, but in his case I made an exception.

Tommy, Aunt Naomi's son, was trying to enlist in the air force. While doing his background check the air force found that Tommy 's name was not Thomas Moles, but John Thomas Strothers and Cleopatra Strothers was his birth mother not Naomi Robinson. Wow! Tommy abruptly discovered my mom was his mom and I was his sister not his cousin. What a mess! Tommy was devastated and hurt no one told him. He was angry with everyone, for not telling him except me because I didn't know either. He went through with the enlistment, left home and volunteered for all foreign duty. He stayed out of the United States for twenty years. The separation from the family never mended his hurt. Tommy said he felt all of them failed him and did not want him in the family. The rest of us changed our last name to Strothers, too, so we would be one, but Tommy never felt like he was a part of us. He kept the Strothers name, but that's all. It had been the other way too long. As expected he remained Aunt Naomi's son even though he recognized he was our brother not cousin. We discussed the fact we all except Mary and Eddie had different fathers but as Mary put it we all came out the same hole so we never spoke of half brother or sister when we were together or when we were separated.

Mom found a nicer place for us to live so we moved to the North Side. I had new friends now and wanted to be with them and wanted to continue go to my same school, but to live better moving was worth it. I decided to ride the street car to school so I never told the school I moved. All was good my problem came when the streetcars went on strike. I lived at least ten miles away from the school. I was determined to get to school so walked up the city steps through Bloomfield and on to Schenley High School. I began walking at 4:00 A.M. and returned home by 6:00 P.M. sometimes 7:00 P.M. I was never late there by 8:00 A.M. and out at 3:00 P.M. Caught pneumonia right as the strike ended but I never missed a day. I had met Billy by then an eleventh grader. He was tall very clean cut, friendly with a big smile. Every time I saw him he was always freshly starched shirt to kakis shoes polished. He was well mannered and used proper English. best of all he had a big smile. We became friends. He walked with me every evening to the street car stop. He stayed after school in detention when I had to stay because I was always in trouble. He was always there I'd look out the principal's office window he'd be looking in. It was uncanny he was always watching out for me. At this time though I was dating Tito, a boy I had known since junior high. Tee and I were a great dance team. He was extremely handsome, a complete gentleman but from time to time a guy would come up to me and say you do know Tito is gay. A fight would break out. I punched anyone who said that girl or guy didn't matter.

One day I was down town passing by Learners on the corner. When I passed these young women talking loud, giggling really being annoying and acting badly. That evening I was at Tee's house so I told Tee about it. I hate ignorant behavior and this upset me so much that young girls could be so obnoxious. He made a gesture like he heard what I was saying but did not respond. Later that week Paul, a guy who I called myself dating before Tee in junior high and I were talking and Tee's name came up. Paul responded, "He's gay." I hit him. That response had happened before and I hit that person, too. I ended up with a black eye both times. When Tee saw me he said what happened to you? I said Paul said you were gay and I hit him. He said Foxy, that's what he called me basically I guess because I had red hair, you need to stop that you're going to get hurt. I said if anyone says you're gay I will hit them.

He said, "Stop fighting, you're going to get hurt. It doesn't matter if people say I'm gay.

I said. "Yes, it does."

He said, "No, it doesn't." He paused and then said, "Because I am. Remember the girls you passed the one who became the loudest as you passed? It was me trying to make you notice. She was me Foxy."

Then by the hand he rushed me upstairs opened a locked closet which held more female clothes than I had. He said these are mine. I was speechless.

I said, "Do your folks know?"

He said, "I don't know, but they were glad about you."

I could tell he was aroused by me We had sex regularly. He dressed impeccably as a male and was quite handsome; except for a few razor bumps on his neck, he was perfect. He had a mustache thin, but nonetheless, a mustache. I was floored.

He said, "I'm a switch hitter. I like men and women, and I can be both." We remained friends, but the romance was immediately over. Wow! Who knew? Guess I was so close I couldn't see. I would have never guessed he was gay. After that night I paid more attention to guy behavior.

Billy kept coming on to me. He even asked me to be his date for the prom. I hesitated because of the cost of gowns and stuff. We did not have extra money for things like proms. Don't know how she did it but Mom as usual came through. She was happy I was going and bought me a beautiful dress. It was a yellow very full hooped skirt gown. Back then girls wore formal gowns to the prom. They were long and wide took up a lot of space. The longer and bigger the skirt the better the gown. My mom was grinning from ear to ear. She had dressed me well. I was a bit disappointed that Billy had on a blue tux. I wanted him to wear a white jacket like the other guys. I later learned that he had to dress himself and the white Jacket was out of his budget. I thought he was better off than he was. We had a good time though. We double dated with his best friend Richard and his girl. It was a great time. We stayed out most of the night but we just had clean fun.

Billy soon graduated and joined the Army. I went to the eleventh grade. Just before he left that morning he came to see me. Mom was at work. Billy and I spent the day saying goodbye on the living room sofa. We hugged, kissed, and soon I found myself rolling out from under him. Billy was finishing basic training when I told my sister I was pregnant. Mary offered abortion. I refused. Mary told Mom I was pregnant and they told Billy's mom. He wrote me and after much wrangling the Red Cross began the effort to get him home from Germany to marry me. Unfortunately, the baby was born a week before he returned home. Mom and I were so broke I lay in the hospital room, wondering how I was going to get clothes to take the baby home. The social worker came in brought me a blanket and gown and Mom and I took the baby home. By that time, I no longer felt the need to marry. I knew Mom could not take care of all of us. I had made this mess so marry I would. In that day it was what was expected. Pregnant not married then get married were all in the same sentence. I don't know. I thought Billy was wonderful and maybe given time I may have wanted to marry him, but now at this time I wanted to go to school to be a doctor. Something about not being able to graduate with my class and having to marry took the oomph right out of the relationship. My mom had her plate full, so I found a razor blade, cut the heels on my black flats straight, put on my paisley blue two-piece suit, and went to get married at the courthouse down town. He and I went to his home where his mom and sisters had prepared dinner for us. Mom came and his brother was there. While waiting for dinner, Billy's mom showed Billy and I to a bedroom where the bed was covered with baby clothes. I laid in the hospital, wondering how I was going to get clothes to take the baby home and his family had all these clothes here. Mom had to ask the social Worker for help because she would not get paid until Friday and they had all these clothes waiting on Billy to get home. I was so hurt. I never said a word, but that was the end for his mom and me. His family thought so little of me that they waited for Billy when I and the baby were in such need. I'm sure no one understood how I felt nor did they care. I was so hurt. I realized, years later, that Billy's family was trying to do the right thing and impress him. His family knew very little about me. To them I was just the girl he got pregnant. They were not aware of how broke I was. Billy told me years later he even thought I had more means, money than he. I know that now but at the time I was seventeen and I didn't understand. I'm certain his mom and sisters were waiting until Billy returned to see the baby in case he said it wasn't his. I said thank you and kept my feelings to myself. I pick my battles there were plenty beautiful clothes, very much needed clothes, so be it. I had gone through the pregnancy without Billy and gotten along okay. Although I needed the clothes I no longer needed him. I just wanted to run away, I knew in reality the baby and I could not make it without help. Mom was working hard enough to take care of me; she did not deserve to be burdened more because of my stupidity. So that was that.

Billy stayed home on leave for two weeks. Just long enough to break a few of my stitches, and then he left for Germany. He had to know I was merely going through the motions cause as hard as I tried I could not feel anything for him.

It wasn't long after he left that I started getting dependent checks. I saved all the money I could, so when he returned we could buy a home somewhere.

I finished high school in a night class and got a GED because I needed Mom to watch the baby while I attended classes. I got the GED because I refused to go another year to get a half semester credit. I got a job working in the diet kitchen at Emerson Hospital and things were going good. Mom still worked but now I was able to take of me and the baby.

Billy was back in Germany and soon began to write every day. He sent gifts and asked for pictures of me and the baby which I sent. I sent pictures of me wrapped a towel in various ways. He liked my red hair, so I made along braid of pubic hair, tied it with a bow, and sent it to him for his wallet. Trying to keep the interest up because we were so far apart. I wasn't dumb enough to think he would not have sex with someone else in two years, but I was surprised he sent me pictures of his shoes under some German girl's bed. Who would believe he would begin writing me about how she cared for him and cried when he left her and went to the barracks. When it was way too late Billy told me he was trying to make me show some emotion. He said, "If I thought there was someone else I would be jealous and act better more excited to be with him." He had the wrong women. What a mistake. He did not know what I had been through with my mother and that trash she married. I was willing to go the distance to make this marriage work. I couldn't believe he was acting like that. I didn't understand it. From that point my effort to be a good wife died. I let all my efforts go to making money. A friend of mine was working as an artist model and seemed to be doing well. She told me about it and said more models were needed. I went for an interview and I got on as a part time model in the evening working for the Carnegie School of Art. The pay was good: $18 every fifteen minutes. Easy as it sounds the catch was I had to pose naked. That took some getting used to. Even worst then being naked in front of people it was very difficult to sit or stand in one position five minutes without scratching or blinking with twenty to thirty pairs of eyes on me. In deed this job was not easy and took a lot of guts, but after a while I learned when to call break and when I could wear a thin drape. After I learned easier ways to sit or stand it got where I could handle the poses.

I was busy taking care of the baby and working, so I stopped worrying about Billy's shoes. On my days off I generally cleaned house. Like most of the neighbors on my street I left a window up to air the house and shake rugs out of. This morning was one of those mornings I was cleaning and the front room window was up. I was sweeping the floor when I heard loud arguing and a guy yelling at someone. I went to the window and looked out and saw this guy kneeling over beating this girl on the ground.

I said, "Stop hitting her!"

He looked up and said, "You want to take her place?"

"A man should not hit a woman!" I yelled. He ignored me, so I grabbed my broom and came out and began to beat him with it.

He stopped and said, "Do you know what she did? She wore clothes I gave her out on a date with another guy."

I said, "Good, you were crazy to buy clothes for someone you are not married to."

While he and I were arguing, the girl jumped up and ran.

He said, "See, now, you will have to take her place."

I said, "And who should I notify about your death?"

He calmed down and we talked awhile then I realizing I was outside in my night clothes, looking terrible.

I said, "If you plan to argue with me, you'll have to come in. I'm not dressed for outside activity."

He followed me in. He seemed like he was really a nice guy just hurt, even though he was just whipping up on a girl. I asked why he had so much oil and dirt on his face. He said he worked on cars and just stopped because he was mad and came to find his girlfriend.

I said, "I was going to fix breakfast; are you hungry?"

He said, "Yeah."

I said, "Go upstairs and wash up, and I'll cook."

He washed his hands and face as much as he could because he was covered in black grease on his face and hands. We had breakfast and he helped me with the dishes. It seemed natural like, like we knew each other a long time. He was so quiet, his eyes followed me not saying much. He smiled but mainly answered what I asked. It should have been awkward being with this stranger I should have never invited in after seeing him beating up a girl outside my window. Oddly enough it was not awkward or strange it felt natural.

The baby woke up. He said, "She yours?" I said yes. He watched me feed the baby and after I fed her I laid down with her to put her back to sleep. He laid down at the foot of the bed with both us. I fell asleep when I woke up. He was gone. I had known this man about four hours didn't know his last name and I was sad he left without saying goodbye. I realized I wanted him there when I woke up. Didn't mean to fall asleep. Crazy right? I thought you look a mess, your married, have a baby and he's gorgeous probable has a dozen women; oh well. I won't see him again and shouldn't.

I started cooking dinner. Mom got home about five o'clock each evening, and I wanted to have dinner done. A knock came at the side door. I answered and there he stood all cleaned up in a black wool and leather sweater and black jeans a clean white face, curly black hair that matched his eyes perfectly cut.

I said, "Hi, I didn't expect to see you again."

He said, "Why you ran my girlfriend off? I told you, you have to take her place."

I said, "I'm married, and I'm sure she will come back. Probably to beat me up for feeding you."

He said, "No, she will not be back and she will not bother you. She is probably grateful you came along to save her; I'd still be beating her."

I said, "You know I'm married, right?" He did not respond. He knocked on the door he left from which was the door in the middle room a few steps in front of where my bed was. We never used that door it was too close to my bed. He stepped in close to me so close I lost my balance and fell backward on the bed. He pulled me back but he fell, too. There we lay him on top of me.

He said, "Hi, I'm Les." He pulled his shirt off over his head and slowly removed my top and shorts, hesitating and waiting for me to say no. I'm sure there was a no in me somewhere, but it did not come out.

I moved closer and gently stroked his hair, and we made love. Not the *it's just sex* kind, which would have been okay at that moment; no this was a takeover. I felt like he was trying to blend us, as if he was marking territory. His moves were strong and intense. Right there, right there held in his grip my body pressed close to his chest feeling every beat of his heart and every movement of his body, I thought, I like the beat of his heart. I want him to need me. I finally felt something for somebody, but it wasn't for the right person.

After that day his ex never returned, and Les left my bed each morning and returned to it at night. We were together each waking moment, either in presence or in thought. In the middle of the day if I was off he would come down the street face oily hands dirty for lunch and to kiss me hello. He was extremely passionate. He could make love in the middle of a snow storm and never feel the cold. This was an unusual man. He did not curse, drink, or smoke. He told me once alcohol made him crazy, so he didn't drink. He would take me to parties but either wait outside or return for me. He did not seem to like mingling with people, either. No other guy would make a pass at me at a party after they met Les. He somehow made it clear not in words because he did not talk much, but in action that I belonged to him. Before he left the room in front of everyone he'd kiss me and walk out. Everyone on the North Side was part of a gang, he was not. I don't know if Les ever felt threatened by anyone because Les sort of had his own gang. He had eleven brothers and a cousin and sometimes they would show a presence walking down the street all together taking up the entire street walking Les to my house. No one knew anything about this family. They did not talk to or date any of the girl on the street. I don't think they approved of Les and me. Can't blame them I was married and they knew. I met his cousin once but none of his brothers ever talked to me. They spoke, said hi but conversation no. I asked Les if it was okay with his family for us to be together he said no. Once his dad came for him as he was leaving he said I've got chores to do I'll be back. He seemed to fear his dad. He moved very quickly to leave. His dad said hello, that's all. His brothers were all stunningly handsome, black hair clear complexions, exotic, tall, and strong-looking. When they walked together, wow—what a sight. It looked like an Indian reservation emptied.

Les was so handy he could do anything and never complained about anything. We were like a married couple. I got so used to being with him that I was shocked when my husband Billy came to the door one evening. Totally by surprise. Billy kept writing about the good time he was having and sending me pictures of him dressed in new suits and in night clubs. I figured this marriage was mutually over. Both of us seemed to have moved on and it was okay. I sent him papers for a divorce now here he was paper's in hand asking why I sent them.

I said, "You are sleeping with a woman in Germany, and you are spending as if you did not plan to have a family or buy a house. I thought this is what you wanted. I said I thought you have moved on I have. I have someone else."

He hit me. Mom must have stopped Les before he got in that night because he did not come. Billy was upset and wanted to know who I was seeing I didn't tell him then Les showed up. There was a big fight. I ended up taking Les to the ER with cuts to his face. I was worried that Less's brothers would come and kill Billy. I forced Les to go home promising I'd be all right. After all of this that night, Billy calmed down and wanted to have sex, so keeping the peace I didn't resist. We were still married and you can't miss what you can't measure. He got released, and I got exercise and time to plan. The next morning, I had it figured it out. I'd make him sick. I prepared a small turkey stuffed with a small amount of Decone rat poison in the dressing. I packed a small bag hid it in the front room. That afternoon I smiled serving Billy dinner. I whispered to Mom not to eat the turkey especially the dressing and to call an ambulance if Billy got sick. I served the turkey greens, macaroni, and cheese with cranberry sauce. While Billy was happily eating, I called a cab, got my bag and the baby, and left for the train station heading for Milwaukee to stay with my sister for a while. Hitting me may happen, but only once. Billy didn't even get a little sick but he did lose a stripe trying to find me. He went AWOL after having car problems getting back to base. Seems he was now stationed at Fort Campbell in the states. With the loss of a stripe he lost pay, and so did I. My check decreased significantly. Leaving town, I thought I didn't care about losing my job at the hospital, but the modeling job I did care about. It paid more. With this in mind I did not plan to stay long in Milwaukee. It was only a temporary haven until Billy left town. I was not going to be one of those army wives who allowed I'll hit you or screw you if I choose because you're powerless. Granted Les and I were wrong, but so was Billy. I filed for divorce I thought he would be glad to be rid of me after all of that. Les and I fought a lot but he never tried to hurt me and I knew it. I had a bad temper, and so did Les right after and usually during the fight, we just stopped fighting and make love on the floor, on the steps, in the kitchen half way under the bed—it didn't matter. Where ever the fight took us. Les would be raggedy and bleeding and I'd be raggedy I'd scratch him he'd rip my shirt or just dump me out of my clothes we fought crazy but it was different. Les never hurt me; he tore the heck out of my clothes, which he promptly replaced with new ones that I chose. I scratched him, tried to bite him, and he'd just confined my arms. If I kicked he laid on me and rubbed his nose softly on my cheek so I couldn't bite him. It was just a different kind of a fight than someone six foot slapping my face and knocking me down.

I finally made it to Milwaukee after changing trains in Chicago, where I thought I'd blow away the wind was so fierce. I was not dressed for that kind of bitter cold. It wasn't much better in Milwaukee. During that winter I froze and when summer came the heat was worst. There was no air conditioning. I was miserable. It was so hot that I spent most of my time in the bath tub filled with cool water. To make things worst I found I was pregnant. Mary was wonderful she tried to make me comfortable, on the other hand she gave her boyfriend, who was there, the blues His name was Rubin. She and Rubin were living together. Rubin worked at night, Mary was out all night. She would sometimes bring the party home in the morning. Loud music, talking loud and Rubin trying to sleep. Don't know how he stood her. He never complained. Rubin was so quiet, so kind I believe Mary could have hit the man with a skillet and if could still stand he would have kept looking at her with that adoring look. I felt so sorry for him. Mary didn't treat him as good he deserved. As much as

Mary and Rubin tried to get me to stay with them I could not. I got a bad tooth ache and the dentist I went to up there could only treat me because I was pregnant he would not pull my tooth. When I returned home after six months I wanted to see Les. It was clear Billy and I would not make it, so I went to my lawyer to see how the divorce was going. Billy still refused to sign the papers. I continued to live as if I were single. My checks were not cut off they kept coming and I used only the money it took to care for the baby and saved the rest. I went back to work modeling. All the agencies loved that they could give their students the opportunity to draw a pregnant figure. I got more jobs than ever but that fame was short lived because I became allergic to the Conti chalk and couldn't work. Besides I was real pregnant by then. It was nearing eight months when one evening I got in unbearable pain. I figured it was labor. I had felt that kind of pain before for twenty-one hours with the first baby, so I packed a bag and got a cab to the hospital. The baby was born about six hours later.

Labor was easier the second time. I didn't get to see the baby. I was told she was very small and was taken upstairs to the preemie nursery right away. The nurse assured me I could see her when I was able to go upstairs. I was not aware that there was a note on my door that directed everyone to stop by the desk before seeing me until Les showed up. I did not want to be in a lurch when it came time to take the baby home, so I had been on the phone ordering baby blankets and clothes. Much of which had been delivered to my hospital room.

Les showed up to visit. He looked around and then said, "What are you doing?"

I said, "There is no one to go shopping. Mom's got the baby, so she has no time to shop. I have nothing to take care of this baby with or take her home in, so I'm ordering stuff from Boggs and Bules."

Les pausing and said, "Irvie, didn't anyone tell you? The baby is dead. It died right after birth. The nurse in the room said we were waiting for your husband to come before we told you. Les said let's go, your leaving."

He began packing my stuff and the nurse said, "Are you her husband?"

He said, "No, but you all let her here three days and don't tell her the baby is dead and she's spending money on all these clothes and stuff. If you got papers to sign to get her out of here, you'd better get them because she's leaving."

Les got a wheelchair put me in it and down the hall we went. The nurse caught up with us at the door and I signed myself out. Sometimes when Les and I were on the mend or it was a hot summer night and we couldn't sleep we'd go to the Hill for a fish sandwich. There was something about that fish sandwich or maybe it was just the ride that always made me feel good.

I must have looked sad cause Les grabbed my hand and said, "Do you want a fish sandwich?"

I said yeah. We drove in his truck to the Hill him glancing at me smiling all the way. We got a fish sandwich.

As we sat eating he said, "You okay?"

I said, "I guess."

He remarked, "It'll take time."

Billy must have found interest in someone else or gave up on me because he finally signed the divorce papers. I was free.

Three years passed and three more to close pregnancies happened. I miscarried all of them. I realized I was having babies too fast and wore a diaphragm but that didn't work because of my shifting weight and breathing disorder. One year I lost a baby in the chamber pot. I remember how I panicked when I felt it coming out and screamed for my mom to come help stop it. There was nothing she could do. I remember the way the fetus looked like a clothes pin just straight and pink and oh the blood. I couldn't have been pregnant more than a month. The other pregnancies were not much different I lost them in bed or walking at three and four months. I had to have a blood transfusion I lost so much blood following the fourth miscarriage. I was seventy-seven pounds and so skinny; that low weight probable did not help. Seventy pounds is the weight at which I was hired for modeling, so I had to maintain a weight close to that to keep my jobs. That was not easy eating apples and salads occasional fish sandwich which after I had to be careful not to eat anything fattening for a while. I got another modeling job with Carnegie Institute Sculpture Division. It paid better but was a harder job because I had to remember one position and hold that pose for a month. It was an everyday job just for a different class. Everything has a purpose I guess.

I had always admired this little house that sat up on the hill overlooking my apartment on Strauss St. It looked like one of those houses in Alice in Wonderland. Long before the house was for sale I knew one day this house would be mine. This house had real charm; I always admired it. It had spades and diamond on the shutters like a deck of cards and it was colorfully painted. It had two bedrooms, living room and a kitchen and a cellar with a room in it. Mainly out of curiosity, I wanted to see the house inside and talk to the realtor to ask the price. I believe he quoted $2,000. After I heard the price, I imagined buying it for a whole week. Two thousand dollars seemed like a good price, but it was quite a bit of money back then. The more I thought about the house and me owning something the more I wanted the house. Yet the thought of buying a house scared me. I wondered if I could afford the payments. I always wanted my mom to have a house of her own, so I wrestled with the idea, lost sleep thinking about it then after a week I took a deep breath went back to the realtor and became a home owner. It felt good to do something on my own. I gave Mom and the baby the bedrooms. I took the room in the cellar. Les and I fixed the space up and it made a fine bedroom with a private entrance. It was wonderful. This was a good year and at the end of it I was pregnant for the sixth time, and this time she lived. I got my job back at the hospital and only worked the modeling jobs as I was available. I had a good friend next door who reminded me often not to put the little baby on the ironing board in her seat while I ironed. I was so afraid something would happen to her I kept my eyes on her a much as possible but the ironing board was a dangerous place, so I listened. I always wanted three children, so now I had two this was good I was happy. People asked why I didn't give up having babies after all that has happened. I said God must have had need of these children because he did not take my uterus or me. I had an almost six-year-old and an eight-month-old and the older was very watchful of the younger. My regular babysitter's children had chickenpox, so I called on my watchful girlfriend who had three kids of her own to watch the kids just for one day. She agreed, so I packed the formula and the cereal and diapers and took the kids next door. I was running late and the baby was crying, so I said to my friend feed the baby her cereal is in the bag and her milk. I was working when I began to feel strange. Someone don't remember who came to tell me to go home the baby was being taken to the hospital. I don't remember how I got there but when I arrived two ambulances were in front of my friend's house. I was quickly put in of those bunk beds. I saw my blankets come out but I could not see the baby. Both ambulance took off for Allegheny General hospital. I could see my blankets being taken into the emergency room from the window before my ambulance came to a full stop I bolted from the ambulance and ran through the hall in the ER trying to find my baby. A policeman or attendant I can't remember which was coming toward me holding my blankets. I couldn't see the baby but I knew Toy was in there. I remember grabbing the blanket and the baby from him. I saw cereal running from her mouth and she wasn't moving. I don't know why I just started running with her in my arms. I must have run a block out of the hospital doors before someone caught up with me and took the baby. I still remember how still she was, and warm. I had on a black trench coat I can't remember how I got home that day. I did though cause right after dark my friend came over to explained what happened. She said she propped the bottle up while she went upstairs to wake her husband for work. Because the older kids chanced waking the baby up she put the baby on the sofa in the living room where it was quiet and made them leave the room. Her sofa had a thick commercial loose plastic cover on it. She added cereal to one of the bottles then slit the nipple in order for the milk and cereal mix to flow better. Toy was eight months old trying to walk, so I think she must have begun to chock on the mixture, pulled on the couch cover to sit up and it covered her face. Phillis said she was only upstairs a few minutes. When she returned the baby was not breathing. This was so hard to hear. I knew she meant no harm, didn't mean to hurt the baby, but what do you say? It's okay, I understand, what? It's been years and I still have no answer.

In the car riding home from the funeral, I wondered why the world was still going on as usual and my world had stopped. I was dazed for a long time after the funeral. For weeks I came in from work every evening made formula and washed the same clean diapers over and over. Mom just let me do it. One evening the bottles were gone. Mom said she's gone Irvie you don't need to making bottles. I went to my room and just sat, I felt or I didn't feel it was like being suspended in space with no direction. It took a long time to wake up, but when I did I knew I could not live next door to Phillis. She was my friend but what could I say to her it's okay, no problem. She still had her kids and mine was gone. I wasn't mad at her but I wasn't ready to move on not yet. I knew this was an accident Phyllis would not intentionally hurt anyone she was a good person and I knew it was a mistake, but I just didn't want to live near or even in the same city with her. Phillis had her three live children and me I was a ball of changing emotion. I tried to heal up. I wanted to move on, but no matter what I did nothing, nothing fixed me. I had to get away and I knew Les would not leave Pittsburgh. I knew that his family ties were too strong for him to leave and his business was rooted there.

Through all the things over the years I put Billy through, he and I were still in communication. When he learned of what happened he called to ask if there was something he could do to help. He suggested I come where he was to get away. I didn't have to think about it long.

For some time I had been asking Les about us moving away but realized he was never going to move or go back to school. I wanted a better life and I wanted to see more than the North Side of Pittsburgh. I was growing but Les was not. This is the life Les knew and he was comfortable in. He was uncomfortable with change. Change bothered me, too, but I had to get out of the dark. I was drowning.

My wish for change came long before this tragedy. Trying to improve myself I applied to a school to become a radiology technician and I was accepted. My first day of school the instructor, a white guy, called me to his desk after class. He said you seem like a nice young lady I like you. You may have what it takes to make it, so I'm going to tell you something. This town does not hire Negros for radiology. If you go to any of the hospitals in this city and find one negro radiology technician I'll take your money. I'd love to teach you, but I don't want to waste your money knowing you won't get a job after your trained. I thanked him for telling me and went about doing what he asked. He was right I went to St. Frances, Allegheny General, St. Mary's, and two to three other hospitals, not one. In Pittsburgh, Pennsylvania, not the south wow, there it was. Yep! He was right. I dropped out of school got a refund and moved on. I still wanted better. The wish for better even got worse when my grade school friend who was marrying the director of the symphony, invited me to her wedding. I missed the wedding subconsciously probable intentionally but made it to the reception. It was fabulous the food, the cake, the atmosphere, oh my and full of people who were definitely out of my league. I didn't stay long I felt strange. I didn't even get to speak with her. There were so many people bubbling around her that I just waved blew her kisses, and mingled toward a side door and left. Won't say I was envious, but I think I kind of was. Not of her because she earned it. She did it right. She went to college finished did all the right things. We make our own choices good or bad. Those choices direct your path. My choices were not healthy the kind that would lead me to a better place in life. Now that I think about it if I had not made some of the mistakes and choices I made at the time I made them I may not have arrived at the mental need to do better as soon as I did. Maybe bad is sometimes good. Right then I felt very small. I only saw my friend once more after that night. She and her husband were in a car down town. He was driving and she was feeding him grapes. Their car slowed beside me. I was standing on a high curb looking down at her. She was turned in her seat facing him and they were talking she looked happy. She didn't see me. I smiled as they drove off.

I needed a new beginning but leaving my mother, who also would not move away, was going to be difficult. She and I had never been apart for a very lengthen time. Then there was Les who was for my teenage years to women my friend my love, my everything. My kitchen, my, bed, my life would be lonely no matter who was in it if not Les but I, needed a change. I couldn't look at Phillis another day, go into my house another day I wanted to scream.

Explaining that I had to leave to Les was awful. He had tears running down his cheeks. He folded and slid down the wall and I held him, I just held him. If I had stabbed him he would have taken the pain better. I never wanted to hurt Les. He never hurt me. I tried to explain We needed to improve our lives and Pittsburgh was not the place to do it. Les did not agree.

I agreed to go to Kentucky and stay with Billy. He said the only way I could stay with him on base is if we were married. Then he said quietly you divorced me too fast without giving me a chance to show what I could do to make our lives better. I was amazed he still wanted to be around me let alone he still loved me knowing all that he knew. The baby I recently lost was not his. All except the first child was not his neither were the other babies except the first. He knew that, too. I wanted a new life, so again, more for convenience than anything, we were remarried at the same courthouse. This time Mom did not go with us. She knew my heart was not in this. I could tell she knew by the look on her face and the dry tone in her always up voice when she congratulated us. Billy thought it was because I was leaving she looked so sad but I knew better. Mom was always on my side. She was my best friend. She knew why I was doing this even if we did not speak about it because she knew me. If this would help me she was for it. I don't care if I told her I'd just murdered someone she'd have said well Irvie what did they do to you? I was her angel and could do no wrong. My mom was my blessing. God gave me a special gift in her.

That day Billy, our daughter, and I left driving to Fort Campbell. The ride must not have been exciting because all I remember about it is looking at the landscape. It was beautiful, tall trees and rocks with water seeping between their cracks giving the rocks glisten in varying shades of brown. As we drove further south, I noticed a change in the color of the dirt. Initially the soil was black then it changed to red. Twelve hours or there about we arrived at gate six Lyons Trailer Court. Before Billy came to get me, he bought a sixty-wide trailer. It was beautiful. There were two bedrooms one on each end of the trailer. The whole thing was new, furniture and all. When Billy went to work the next day I began to making this trailer our home. I put my daughter in the bedroom at the front of the trailer and made the back bedroom ours.

The following day after Billy left for work a knock came at the door and in walked Jackie. My life has never been the same. She was wildly outspoken, uninhibited, and classy.

She said, "I live next door. I'm glad you're here. You are from up north, right?"

I said, "Yeah."

She said, "You need some clothes. We need to go shopping." That was the beginning. The Davis shop got to know us well. The first thing I bought was a feedbag pure leather bag. After that my outlook and entire wardrobe changed. Jackie and I spent much of our day in the base craft shop making it home in time for our kids to get in from school and to cook. I wanted to work, but Billy said no he wanted me home cooking. Don't know why because he liked country cooking and I was not too good at country. Once I was looking out our back window and saw what I thought was cabbage over in a field drying out going to seed. I got me a big bag and went out and cut some of the leaves down. I brought them home washed each leaf cut them up and put ham hocks in the pot put a lid on it and cooked them all day slow. These cabbage had a stranger smell than usual, but I figured it was because they had been out in the sun too long.

Billy came home and said, "What's that smell?"

I told him I'd cut some of the cabbage leaves down from the farm behind us since the farmer didn't care he was letting the plants go to seed and I was cooking them.

He pointed at the plants from the window and said, "Those leaves?"

I said, "Yeah."

As he dumped the whole pot in the toilet, he said, "That man's going to get you about his tobacco." We went out to eat that evening while the house aired.

Shopping was expensive and spending my days at the craft shop was getting boring. I wanted to go to school but when I tried talking to Billy about it he laughed. I told him I wanted to be a doctor. He really laughed. He told me way later in life that he didn't think I was smart enough to become a doctor. Can't blame him the way I acted when we were in school didn't show much intelligence. There was reason for that behavior. Mom wanted me to go to college, but I knew we could not afford it, so I acted unsmart as if education wasn't important. I had no idea I could have gotten a loan or grant and gone. No one told me. Things you don't know wow. My goals had not changed. I'd grown and education was important to me. Back then a female as a doctor was not something most people took serious. The options for women were get a good husband, become a teacher, or a secretary. Even the counselors in guidance lead girls to believe this was all there was. Mothers would tell a girl a man wants a good wife, dinner on the table, someone to roll in the hay with when he got home and if you give him a son you'll see things will be fine. Never mind the women was home going brain dead and wanting a life too.

It was all about pleasing the man. I was growing weary of wifely chores. I wanted a pencil and a book.

I couldn't go to school, so I had to do something. I got a job as a waitress in the Elks Club. Jackie worked there and she got me on. Of course we worked at night and no husband would like that. It was a fun job. The music was live and the place was rocking. Soldiers were everywhere I could put my serving tray down and dance. This was a night life I hadn't seen much of. I loved it. Neither Les or I drank the only clubs I went to were where artist like Wilson Pickett or Bo Diddle were performing in person. Then I stayed only long enough to hear them sing cause if you don't drink no one wants you to take up a seat. My job was short lived cause Billy didn't want me working and defiantly not till 3:00 A.M. and not in a club. The tips were great and helped our budget especially since I had become a shopaholic. I had my own money I could help. I was spending crazy. I changed all the furniture in the living room down to the carpet and added an entertainment center. I bought a tangerine colored carpet. Had it put down the morning I bought it. It was a-mazing it made the whole room perk up. I had the best looking trailer in the court. Billy came home every day peeping through the window to see if I had changed the house again. He said he had to check to be sure he had the right house. He never complained about my spending. He complained about my job and made me quit. Since he made me quit I kept buying. He'd say what did you buy today and how much debt am I in? Got to say he was patient.

Since I had to quit my job and Jackie did not want to drive home from Clarksville to Gate six alone at 3:00 A.M. she quit, too. There we were jobless but we didn't go broke. Jackie and I had gained quite a few admirers who got joy out of spending their money on us. They were retired soldiers who were home all day and were used to preying on soldier's wives. I'm sure for money a few of these women would lay with them all day cause most of the time soldiers and their wives are broke. I'm sure some of the wives slept with them during the day and were home by 4:00 P.M. to cook supper. Some used a crock pot and dinner was on, and so were they. Believing we would deliver when our husbands were in the field like some of the other wives they handed money out very freely. We never delivered we had a million excuses to stall. We were ahead of the game and went in knowing who was doing who. When our husbands were in the field she and I went to many of the parties, had loads of fun keeping hope alive and not delivering anything. I could write a page on the excuses we had for getting out of things. Jackie and I were coordinated we came together and left together and we were never broke. There is a saying that I don't think those schemers had heard. Jackie and I had, if you find a fool bump his head and we did. Believe me there are plenty of hawks around a military base.

Idle time is not good I don't remember how the subject came up but I think I mentioned to Billy we should try for another baby if I was going to be home anyway. Eventually I thought he would consider me going to school to take maybe one or two classes since we were near Austin Peay College. So, I thought okay, let's do the family thing now and be free when it was time for daycare later. He said no. I don't want any more children with you. I said why? He said I just don't. That hurt my feelings, but I was used to it when Billy was not being nice he was being mean. He never expressed it but I knew he still held malice cause of the things I did in the past. He should have let me stay in Pittsburgh. If he would have said we can't afford a baby I would have understood, but this attitude seemed strange to me since he frequently accused me of being gay because I didn't want to have sex every night and morning. I was definitely not gay. I didn't want to hurt his feelings since I heard his sisters tease him about the oversize of his penis in front of me and it bothered him to the point of anger. I knew he was embarrassed by it, so I never said anything, but it was true he was excessively endowed and grossly under skilled, so sex with him was not pleasing and left me sore for days sometimes. The fiddle was super great, but the maestro was clumsy and tone deaf. It was my mistake. I never told him, so we never discussed it. I figured he should have seen the pain on my face and asked am I hurting you. He never asked. I'm sure he knew there was a problem and didn't care. Maybe because he didn't know how to fix it. Maybe I should have bought him a how-to manual.

The relationship between Billy and I was never strong but the little we had was deteriorating. Billy was mad at me a lot because when we went to his friend's house for gatherings I wouldn't drink. He said it was an insult. He and his friends all loved bowling and beer. I hated it and they smoked cigars I hated that too. I did not smoke or drink and did not want to be around a bunch of drunk smokers unless I was being paid to serve the drinks. He and I rarely talked. I cooked and kept the house clean but the marriage needed a shine. Don't know what got into Billy but he wouldn't let me drive my car or his. Looking back, he probably feared me getting a ticket on base cause the soldier not the spouse was made to go to school and was reprimanded for the mistakes of the driver no matter it was not the soldier driving. That policy caused many wives to get beating by their husbands. Those guys lost stripes after their wives got tickets. They would go home and beat the crap out of their wife.

No school, no baby; I was so bored I got another job in another club waiting tables only on Friday and Saturdays and this time I didn't quit.

Working took up some of the boredom. It beat the bowling alley and Billy's drunk buddies and their puppet wives. There was a handsome man who wore sun glasses all the time to whom I used to serve scotch and water. When he saw me coming with his tray he would sort of block the table turn facing me with his legs spread and arms out, so I had to get close to him to place the drinks on the table. I was use to nuts and could handle the crazies very well. If they got too touchy feely I had two bouncers as back up. He was just playful and never touched me. I never saw him drunk and never smoking. One night as the crystal ball was spinning and strode lights were flashing I was serving his table as I came close to his table he turned like usual and removed his glasses. I almost dropped the drinks. I'd never seen a person who's eyes reflected yellow like a dog or cat. He must have known I would react like that because he grabbed the tray. I apologized almost spilling ice and scotch on his beautiful suit.

He said, "I'm Donnie; sorry I scared you."

I couldn't lie. I said, "Your eyes are different but pretty. They look like dog eyes."

He said, "Birthmark."

I said, "Is that why you wear those glasses in the dark?"

He said, "Yes, I don't want to scare people. I don't wear them all the time. During the day my eyes look normal; they just reflect light at night."

Donnie was always in the club when I was. He would lean on the bar or wait until I served his table and ask me to dance. He was so smooth he looked good and he smelled like Jade East. I loved to smell of him. A lot of the soldiers were just lonely had five kids at home and a wife and fed women who would listen a bunch of bull, so when he began with the "I want to know you better" line, I said, "Yeah, yeah, I'm married."

He said, "Yeah, yeah, I know. I'm not."

He did fool me, though; one night at closing Donnie was knocked out on his table. This was new I served him drinks but to that night I had not really even seen him drink over a sip usually over lots of ice. His friends drank the most. I tried to get him up, but he was too out of it to drive. I didn't know what to do with him I couldn't take him home and I didn't want the hookers to take his wallet, so I got a cab and took him to a local hotel, got him in the room and on the bed and he woke up, pulled my arm and said stay, in that melt you in your underwear voice.

He removed his glasses and said, "I'm not drunk." He pulled me in bed with him. I stayed. Billy was away for the weekend and I had a sitter. I enjoyed hearing nice things for a change whether he meant them or not. I was sick of being verbally beaten up. Donnie was gentle and warm and by the way far from drunk. He faked all of that to see what I would do. He had a golden, well-built body that could melt ice from across the room. I could have remained laying near him talking, laughing forever. He was fun and his kisses were incredible. I found out he drank very little and was ordering drinks and giving them to his friends, so I would return to his table. That night he told his guys to leave him. He was not asleep or drunk. He said it started as a joke, but the more concerned I became the more he wanted to see what I would do with him. That night was beautiful. I hated it had to end. It was worth every minute to me.

Didn't think I could work at the club and see him with someone else next week, but I was married and he was free and if you have sex with a stranger from a bar that's what you get. I thought I would probable only see him in the club, the chase was over he got what he wanted, so he would do what all good hunters do after the kill look for new game. I prepared myself to quit if Donnie was with someone else. I was not able to look at him with someone else.

I went to work the next weekend. He wasn't there. Don't know if I wanted to see him more than I didn't want to see him at all or what. I just wanted to stand and scream I was so confused. A little after midnight he walked in alone which he never did. I was embarrassed to face him. I felt like street trash, so I avoided his table. He sat staring at me not ordering from the other waitresses. He shooed them off. After about an hour my boss came over to me and said one of the customers complained that I was ignoring his table pointing to the table where a women and Donnie were sitting. He said fix the problem.

I gathered myself went over to the table and said, "What can I get you?"

"Why are you avoiding me?" he asked.

I said, "I have been busy. I apologize; I can take your orders now."

He said, "That's not true. I have watched you for an hour. and you have acted like you don't see me. What did I do? Why are you upset with me?"

I started to look at the lady sitting at his table. He said, "I asked you a question."

I said, "I'm working."

He said, "I'll wait." I walked away and he followed me and said, "I'm sorry, can you get this lady a scotch neat?"

I said, "What about you?"

He said, "I'll take you without the ice."

I said, "She's going to be mad if you don't go back and sit down."

He said, "That's my table she was sitting at. I'm not with her unless you want me to be. I'm here because of you."

I had an awful week—couldn't sleep, couldn't function almost got killed on the gun range. I want us to be together. I said I'm married. He said I can fix that. He reached in his pocket and then opened his hand and was holding my underwear.

He said, "I looked your husband up and started to give him these, but I didn't want him to hurt you. Can we talk after you get off?"

I said, "Only for a little while. Give me those."

He closed his hand and said, "Only if I can put them where they should be."

We met after work and our talk became a passionate hour. After that our talks were quiet. We spent little time discussing work of the day or the people we knew we just made love every chance we got. Billy made me quit the club, so I didn't see Donnie much. I did enroll in college, but after a few classes Billy wanted me to quit that too. He said a working women made her high and mighty college made her worse. I was determined to stay in school. He was insistent, so I agreed after this one quarter.

As it came time to enroll again, I talked to Billy about staying even to just take dance. He said no. I needed to be home.

I went to talk with Jackie about it.

I said, "I can't stay there; I'm miserable. There's no love in this house and nothing I do will make Billy happy unless he is pushing me through the mattress every night or I'm cooking a three course meal with a bottle of beer in one hand and a bowling ball in the other while puffin on a cigar. I've had it."

She said, "Where will you go?"

I said, "I don't know. I don't have enough money to survive alone."

She said, "Call Donnie; he's so in love."

I said, "Until I need him, most likely."

I called Donnie. He didn't answer, so I left a message. The morning and afternoon all day passed and no answer.

About six o'clock, in walked Donnie to pick me and my daughter up. He said, "Let's go."

I said, "I don't have any money or anywhere to stay."

He said, "You said that; let's go and yes, you do. I got us a place today and you have me. Don't worry about money."

I said, "I thought you wouldn't come."

He said, "I was at work. Sure, I was coming. I live on base in the barracks and had nowhere to take you, so when I got off I needed time to rent something off base. I wanted some were to take you when I came. Didn't want to just drive around."

He was true to his word. The apartment was fully furnished and very nice. He said, "When you feel like it, you can ditch the furniture and get what you like. This is temporary. We need a house. I'm starving I'll bet the baby is too let's go eat. We'll shop for groceries later."

He pulled me to him hugged me picked up the baby, as he called her, hugged us and said, "It'll be all right, you'll see."

I began working every night and enrolled in school three days a week. Donnie was so grateful to have someone to come home to and cook for him. He loved to eat and I liked to cook. It was perfect. I never saw him frown, and never heard him speak loud. He liked it that I was in school. He was so different, so happy. He sort of danced his way through the apartment and sang I'm going to wait till the midnight hour till my love come tumbling down all the time when showering, walking through the house and especially when he was holding me. This was a happy man. He made me happy, too. I would put his tee shirts under my pillow when he had to be gone overnight, so I could smell him. Everything he wore smelled like Jade East cologne and I loved it. Even gone one night I would cuddle with his shirt or drape his sock over my head to have him near. One night without him was a long, long time. I missed him terrible. He was so sweet. I knew he had another side I made no mistake about it I'd seen him handle those who thought he could be pushed, but to me he was as gentle as can be. You would think he thought I would break I had it all. Donnie cared for all my needs even before I knew I had them. No more parties for me when Mel and Donnie were in the field Jackie came up, she hated to be alone, and we would have talked and shop all day but that was it. If Donnie was home when I left the house with Jackie, he would get quiet. He always acted as if this was the last time he would see me. He'd hug me and say please come back I'll be lonely till you do. He would kiss me and put a hundred-dollar bill in my bra and say buy something for the midnight hour. He'd tell Jackie drive safe ye haul precious cargo. I've learned to live without lots of things, but I won't make it without her. That's the way it was. We lived on Paradise Hill and often I thought it was aptly named cause certainly I was in paradise. I filed for divorce again and struggled to find grounds because Billy was a good person, and father. I just didn't love him. It couldn't have been easy for him cause I'm sure he knew it. The problem was we wanted different things. Billy wanted a housewife and I wanted a career. He thought he could change me and I thought he was more leant than he was. Mistake one we should have remained friends and not married at all especially the second time. It just wasn't there for us. He was a good person he deserved a good wife one who had the same mind set as he. Billy wanted someone I wasn't. I would never be satisfied being home all day anticipating his every need. I wanted more from life than that. That's why I left Pittsburgh and the life I knew.

The Vietnam conflict was starting The guys were having their wives dye their tee shirts green. On and off base you could see clothes line after line green tee shirts flew in the breeze. This was the beginning of troops being deployed to Vietnam. Billy said he had no reason to be here, so he volunteered. He came by the apartment one night and brought my clothes and asked where to send the furniture. He handed me the signed divorce papers and left. I hated to see him look so defeated. He said, "You look happy. I wish I could have done that." Why is it that there is always such a big price for happiness? He made me sad. Billy was a good guy I never meant to hurt him. I hate my happiness came at his hurt. The beginning was all wrong. I don't advise anyone to marry cause of pregnancy. True in this case the baby was helped by the support cause alone I could not have afforded her care but look what trauma it cost.

Not long after that my happiness end. Donnie became a short timer scheduled to get out or re-up. Everyone knew the conflict in Vietnam was growing into a war and after a while all discharges would be held. Donnie and I discussed it and he opted to get out while he could. He did not want to be a career soldier. I was sure we were going home together, but he said he would go get a job with Otis Elevator and send for me when he had everything set.

I said, "I can go. I'll get a job and help out until we're on our feet."

He said, "No, I have to stay with my mother until I'm straight and she would not allow us to stay together." Then he said the words that have motivated everything I have done since. "What can you do?"

I said, "I can wait tables or model for an art school."

He said, "My mom would die if she knew I dated anyone who worked in a bar and I can't let you work as an artist model. I'll send for you when I can take care of us."

When the day came for Donnie to leave and he closed the door started walking toward the cab it was as if my heart was being squeezed and pulled out. It crossed my mind to lay in front of his cab to stop it from moving. Maybe it would show Donnie how crazy I felt and how much I needed him. I was devastated even thinking about living without Donnie. I didn't know how I would. I wish I had the words to explain how I felt when Donnie got in that cab and I stood helpless to make him stay. I watched as my heart roll down the street. It was worse than death in death you know it's final there is no returning, but in an "I'll send for you" all you're left with is when?

For hours that morning, I sat in the quiet of our apartment. I thought about what had just happened. I vowed to myself no one would ever ask me what I could do again and I not have a detailed list of professional answers. Donnie saying that made me even more determined to go to school and get a profession. I never realized that waiting tables in a bar was such a low class and looked down on job. I was a good waitress and I made an honest living. I knew Donnie's mom had a big influence on his behavior, so it came as little surprise he highly considered what she thought. A while ago before he left his mom called me on the phone and asked did I know how old Donnie was. I said no. She said he's nineteen. He was an E-5 that's a big rank for a nineteen-year-old. He had a knack for money a thriving business money lending never broke, physically strong, and very responsible. No one no one messed with Donnie. He was strong, confident and smart. I believe he loaned money for a fee to those who needed a quick loan. He handled crisis well. He took on a readymade family and handled it. My daughter and I loved him. I never considered his age. I never asked. He looked twenty-five, at least. She said he put his age up to enlist and he is nineteen. Donnie had a scar from his eyebrow to his cheek. Which he later told me was from a milk bottle hitting him in the face when he through it up in the air as a child. He had this deep red, rough complexion. There was no child about him. He had no features of any nineteen-year-old I'd ever met. If he was nineteen I was twenty-three and definitely older than him. She said you're too old for him. I gave the phone to Donnie so they could sort it out. I didn't want to do anything to upset him. I didn't care if he was twelve and I was twenty-eight I was not leaving him unless he said so. I wanted to tell her he is good now think I'll stick around until he's forty and experience the improvement, but I didn't. I understood her concern if my son was away dating someone I didn't know and she was older than him I would be concerned too. After all, because of their loneliness some women around base take a soldier to the cleaners every day. I gave the phone to Donnie and walked out of the room. I could feel his anxiety as he was trying to take the phone from my hand. I watched his teeth clinch and his face getting redder. I heard him say, "Why did you tell her that?"

That was the last I heard of it they talked awhile. He quietly put the phone down, walked in the kitchen, put his arms around my waist, and started to sing in my ear. I'm going to wait till the midnight hour kissed my cheek and went upstairs. I kept fixing dinner. I could hear the water running. I knew he was bathing. I turned everything cooking down and went upstairs to wash his back. I removed my shoes and straddled the back of the tub and his back and began to wash his skin. He turned around and pulled me in under him we made love in the tub. Donnie and I never needed many words to express what we felt each of us just knew. He rarely explained anything. He was what he was. That was Donnie. Maybe he was nineteen, I never asked and he never said. The song had ended it was quiet, he was gone.

I kept on working at the club and sleeping with his tee shirt. The smell of him kept me sane. I had to get another part time job washing clothes for two soldiers and cleaning their house twice a week when I wasn't in class. This was good The child support checks hadn't begun, so we made do. It was fine. Months went by Donnie and I talked on the phone and wrote each other often. After about a year I began to wonder if we would ever be together. I took up friendship with a handsome guy a bit older than me who worked at a local factory. He got off work about 11:00 P.M. and always stopped in the club right after. We made friends. We talked about life this, that, and the other nothing romantic. He started driving me home after I got off. Said it was on his way no need for me to walk when the bartender couldn't drive me it was too dangerous. We were talking one night and he said I sleep most of the day then I work why don't you drive my car to work during the day just drop me at home. I said you sure. He said it just sits and you need it. He said I have another ride to work. I said yeah that would be great.

I forgot to remind me to remember nothing is free. He and I became close. I liked him. He said his wife died and he was raising two girls alone with some help from their grandmother. During the day his mother-in- law watched them. He explained she hadn't gotten over his wife dying and would not like seeing anyone driving her car, so stay off Sharon Street if I could. Not a problem it was not on my way to Kentucky or to the club. He said tell you what you keep the car I'll just drive my truck to work. Let's call him Animal. Animal began to come over with groceries and I'd cook and he would nap till it was time to go to work. One day I was home sick and he came and got in bed with me. We were in bed the whole day. I don't know where he found energy to work that night. I showed him what a young girl could do. That was one of many days. He slept there many nights too. I always made him leave before my daughter got up. He was no Donnie, but I didn't think Donnie was going to send for me it had been well over a year nearer two since I even considered talking to or going out with another man. Animal and I were okay. I cared about him not wild crazy but okay. He was wild about me though and extremely jealous. Guys in the club would ask what did you do to Animal he's changed. He watches you like we're going to steal you. I use to tease him I'd say a jealous man can't work. He'd laugh. He was quiet not easily shaken a nice guy. I was driving his car down the street one day and a brick hit my back window. Thinking I'd gotten into a bad neighborhood I didn't stop until I got home. I said, oh my Animal's going to kill me when he sees this. When Animal came in the club that night and I took him out to see the broken glass in the rear of the car.

He said "Where were you?"

I said, "I don't know I didn't stop to check the signs it scared me so bad."

He said, "Okay, no problem. I'll have it fixed."

I said, "I'll help pay for it."

He said, "It's okay."

That was Thursday. On Friday night, I came to work and Gerald, the bartender, said, "Animal's ole lady is over there be careful."

I said, "He's not married; his wife has been dead thirteen years."

He said, "Well, she must have kicked all the dirt off her because she's over there with the manager's wife."

I went over to the table to see and asked, "Would you like to order?" Both ladies said no. I was looking to see if I saw a wedding ring on her hand. I didn't see one. I went back to the bar and said, "Everyone knows I date Animal; why didn't someone tell me he had a wife?"

Gerald said, "Figured you knew; don't get into other folks' business."

Didn't make much difference that he was married in this town everybody cheated when they could. That's the way it was. I made an effort to stay out of her way all evening. I never turned my back on her though. That I didn't do. I figured she knew about me or she would not be here and if she threw that brick she was not above hurting me. Animal usually came in the club around midnight with a big smile and outstretched arm for me to greet him with a kiss. Tonight, no difference. I hugged him and instead of kissing him on the cheek I whispered your wife is behind me. Animal was dark complected but I believe he turned a little blue. He opened his eyes dropped his arms and walked over to her table. She began to scream at him. It got real loud. I went to the bar told Gerald I was leaving counted my purse turned it in and left. About 2:00 A.M., Animal was at my door, knocking.

I said, "Go home."

He said, "Let me in."

I said, "Go home." All of a sudden he kicked the door open.

I said, "You're paying for that."

He tried to explain that his wife had not wanted to leave the house for thirteen years. He said they were not in love just married. He'd leave he wanted me. He stayed cause of the children yada, yada, yada, on and on. Morning was coming, so I persuaded him to leave because my daughter was waking up. He didn't want to but finally he left. I quickly packed our things paid the rent lady next door. Got a cab to the Greyhound bus station got a ticket for Pittsburgh and left.

About fifteen minutes into the ride, the bus stopped on the street and Animal boarded. He rode with me all the way to Bowling Green, begging me to come back. "I'll get a divorce. I'm sorry, whatever you want." I cared for Animal, but not enough to have him give up his family. I don't break up families. He and I were fun, not future. It wasn't that he cheated that bothered me. It was if they do it with you they will do it to you. No thanks. He and I were good because I was lonely. Guess we both were. I wasn't lonely anymore I was cured. He got off the bus I kept going.

Here I was in Pittsburgh again. I thought I'd feel the same about being home but being home was different. In my mind this was where home was, but in my heart home had changed its zip code. It was summer school was out the kids were playing everything seemed as it was. The scenery had not changed. My friends were doing the same things Tonya one of my good friend and the group still played cards all day on her porch. There was still drama. Her husband, fresh out of jail, had gotten the sixteen-year-old next door pregnant. The baby looked just like their daughter. Even though he had recently gotten out of jail he was now accused of messing with another young girl at his daughter's sleep over and Tonya still lived with this piece of crap. Another friend recently died of a heart attack her husband went to work she was in bed with indigestion he gave her medicine. He returned that evening she was still in bed Maalox on her lips dead. I felt like a stranger as if I was watching one of those daytime soap opera where if you don't watch for a year you really haven't much to catch up on because nothing really changes. I didn't really share interest with any of my friends anymore. Days here were dull. No one seemed to care that they were not doing anything positive. I was ready to go right back to Tennessee. It was great seeing Mom I missed her. I didn't see Les at all. Didn't look for him. No need in getting involved with his life. Gerald, called and said we miss you why don't you come home. I said I want to but I have no money. He said where do I send it. I told him, he mailed a ticket and money and I left. This time because I wasn't sure where I was going to stay I left my daughter in Pittsburgh with my mom. I can stay anywhere but I didn't know what the circumstances would be or where I would be living, so it was best not to drag my child through that. She needed to be safe. The apartment was gone and at this point I couldn't afford the rent anyway. It was summer I figured I would be stable by fall and able to come get her before school started. Mom enjoyed being with her granddaughter anyway and I needed time to regroup. My plan was to stay with Jackie for a while, but I fell asleep and missed my stop and I ended up in Clarksville at the bus station which was closed. I phoned Jackie to come get me but her answering machine said she and her husband were out of town on R and R. So now I have nowhere to stay and one quarter to my name. There was one cab left there. I asked him to wait. I dropped my last quarter into the pay phone and called the DAV club asked for Gerald. I said I have nowhere to stay and no more money. He said get a cab and come here. I arrived there no luggage it was in the bus station and it was closed. Gerald handed me a tray and said we'll work on you when we close. When we got all the glasses washed money counted and the chairs put up on the tables for the cleaning crew we left. He and his friend drove me to the Greenwood Inn. I knew this place Donnie and I had spent many precious nights there. Just this once I thought someone was being nice to me for no reason I should have known better. To whom anything is given much more is expected especially if it is given by a man. Gerald was not a bad guy just a guy with opportunity. Having the advantage somehow often lead a good guy to take advantage of a situation. I let my guard down forgetting men are innate hunters. I became pry. We were only in the room a few minutes sitting on the bed watching T.V. and talking. Gerald began to rub me on my thigh. I said stop and scooted away up toward the pillows then his friend grabbed and held my arms and Gerald pulled me out of my pants and underwear. His friend pulled me out of my shirt and bra. Gerald spread my legs, lowered his pants and entered me. His friend straddled my head and held me down while Gerald forced himself in me by pushed until it happened. I didn't scream because they threatened to put something in my mouth if I did. I fought like a tiger it took both of them to wear me down but in the end I was raped all night. Getting raped is awful, but in the end it's just sex and not worth smothering or getting more hurt over. A cat enjoys toying with a moving mouse the more it struggles the more fun it is for the cat and the more danger to the mouse. Gerald didn't let his friend have me but they both thought this was fun and took their time touching and squeezing me everywhere. They had the advantage and took it. This was frightening, disappointing and embarrassing, but it was over and only one night. I knew I had to depend on Gerald and he did too. I had no money and nowhere to go. I had to look at it as payment in return for helping me begin again. I didn't see this as any different from being a housewife without a job. You get used to being used to pay for your keep. The only difference, a marriage license makes it legal and a responsibility. Been there done that.

No matter how bad the night morning eventually comes. Gerald decided until I could afford a place I would sleep in the back room at the club. It was behind the bar had a bed it was a private room with a door no one used it. I didn't know the room was there. It was fine at least after work I didn't have to make my way home so late at night. These arrangements worked out well other than waking up with Gerald in my bed some mornings. I thought the first night he attacked me took care of my debt but guess not. It became a routine and never stopped it turned into friends with benefits. I had saved money now cause my tips were pretty good I averaged $100-$200 a night even more on Friday and Saturday nights. This was a wild time soldiers leaving for the war drinking to avoid thinking about it. Just throwing money away. Sometimes they would give me a hundred-dollar bill get forty dollars' worth of liquor and say keep the change. I use to try to tell them the change was too much but trying to impress some women they would just wave me away. I figured the next day they would miss the money, so I started to keep the money and tag it with a name. The next time I saw them sober I would say I think I owe you some money and give it back. It got to the point word of mouth most soldiers looked for me to give their wallet to and to wait their table. Drunk and trying to impress a woman they usually tipped way too much. When I saved their butts gave the tip back the next night they still gave me ten or twenty dollar tips for returning their money. Something else happened too. The hookers would take them on a date and take their wallet. I use to warn the guys, so when they started to drink some of them would come to me count out what they would keep and give me the rest of their money in the wallet. I'd give them a ticket with a balance on it and their ID this with the understanding that I would under no circumstances give this wallet back that night. I charged $20 for wallet rescue. Had quite a few customers. I got to know the Hookers too. Guys who didn't know who was a working girl and who was not would ask me. I would point them to Short Brenda. She would tip me after the date. The other girls came to me and asked why do you give the guys all to short Brenda? I said she tips me well after the date. They said why didn't you say so, we'll tip you, too. After that I pointed at whoever was not busy. My savings increased dramatically. I didn't register myself for school again because I wanted to be stable and get my daughter back and us to be in our own place first. Make no mistake about it I had not given up on college. I just had to get priorities straight. Situation being as it was I still liked being there better than in Pittsburgh. I was saving and able to send money home to Mom. I was having fun too. Sunday nights were especially fun. It was the only night many bartenders and waitresses were off from work. It was their night to get together and have fun. We would drive up to the Elks in Guthrie. The place was wild. Everyone was dressed to the nines, shaking hands, hugging. I guess it felt like wow were free tonight don't have to wait on anyone tonight. It was fun just being out dancing.

The music was fantastic and since it was only open to waiters, bartenders, club owners, Pimps and Players who frequented and supported the clubs we all understood each other. There were no arguments and no fights just over the top drinking and live bands dancing and singers. I remember one night my purse, in which I always carried a gun, fell off the toilet paper roll in the bathroom hit the floor and bullets flew. No one was hurt but I ruined a good purse. I had the safety on but somehow it released. Man did that scare me. No one else seemed to notice. The music was so loud I don't guess anyone heard the shots. It was a different time. A time when people were used to gun shots. No one panicked because usually no one shot into a crowd. If you were being shot at the shooter would walk up to you and shoot. It's possible that even if someone got shot on the dance floor no one there would stop dancing. They would think the victim passed out drunk and unless they saw blood just dance around the body. Me, I got a new gun never carried that one again.

I never realized that after the club closed the atmosphere changed. The club gained a new life once it closed to the public. About 3:00 A.M. it turned into a private gambling spot. New faces and big money was flowing. I could not see the voices but I could hear them from behind the wall. Some nights, things got real intense. So much so I laid there thinking If someone shoots a gun at a wall I may be killed. I wanted to move my bed from the line of fire but there was nowhere to move it.

I hadn't discussed this with Gerald cause where else was I to go, but much to my surprise and delight one morning Gerald came in and said we have to move you your too close to the gambling. If they got to shooting over there your apt to catch a bullet. I think he remained the bartender even after hours and he knew the danger.

He said, "I found you a place. Get your stuff."

He took me over to this nice house. It had two bedrooms living room and kitchen with a generous back yard. The lady who's house it was said, "How much can you pay now? It's fifty dollars a month. That's your bedroom pointing to the right and you can use the rest of the house this is my room stay out of it."

My room was furnished nicely and the rest of the house was clean and rather nice. I thought this was a good arrangement but still not the environment I want when I bring my daughter back. The house was close to work, had seemingly good neighbors and I could afford the rent. I paid her she gave me a key and vanished. I rarely saw Eartha, my land lord or her husband. Things were going good I had a place to cook and was able to buy food at the base, so I use to stock up on groceries. I cooked every day. I noticed my left overs were disappearing. For a while I kept it up, but it got expensive cooking for three, so I stopped cooking. Eartha's husband, JC, came to me said, "Why aren't you cooking?" I told him I just couldn't afford to buy groceries every week and cooking for all of us was expensive. I couldn't afford it. He said, "How much does it cost to cook for all of us?"

I said, "About a hundred dollars."

He said, Eartha cannot cook, you know."

I said no I didn't. He reached in his pocket and handed me a one-hundred-dollar bill and said, "Keep cooking."

Every week he would give me a hundred dollars and I would cook the best meals desert and all. Eartha was happy she didn't have to go near the kitchen. JC was thrilled and I put $25-$30 in my stash each week. Eartha was either out or asleep, so I rarely saw her. JB was rarely there, so I saw him even less. I pretty much had the house to myself. When I got home from working my day job I cooked and went to bed until 9:00 P.M., got up and went to work at the club by 10:00 PM. Saturdays is when JB was there all of us usually managed to meet in the kitchen. Once JB had these people, two women and a man, staying over the weekend. They were strange. I couldn't get over how two women were almost fighting to wash this man's clothes and wait on him hand and foot. These women took turns rubbing his back, arms and every other body part they could rub. Sometimes they did it in harmony. They didn't even care that I saw them. The door was open. They both slept with him one on the right and the other on the left both having sex with him one at a time or both at a time. These were not ordinary people he was a pimp with two of his top girls and both of them were vying to be his number one girl. Each of them doing the best she could to please him. JB said we could do that. I could make lots of money with you. I thought he was kidding at the time, so I gave him a nasty look and moved on. Not too long after that I found out he was not kidding. Eartha always told me I was so green if they threw me over in a field the cows would eat me up. I was not as green as she thought I was. I realized more than she thought. I was quiet and observant, but not oblivious to what the people around me were like. In one way I was smarter than her. She trusted JB for all her needs when she should have gone to school and gotten an education and become independent making a better life for herself. She was pretty and tall she could have found a man who respected her more.

One morning I woke up and walked to the kitchen and Eartha's bedroom door was cracked not enough for me to see in, but open. JB was gone, so he may have left the door open. This was odd I never passed her door a jarred. I didn't dare touch the door, so I just went on with my day came home and the door was still cracked like it was. I went to bed got up went to work at the club and when I got home at 3:00 A.M. the door remained the same. I thought maybe Eartha left in a hurry and the door did not shut. I didn't look in I thought, maybe it's a trick to see if I go in her room while she's out. I went to bed. The next morning, I was cleaning up when I thought I heard a noise coming from Eartha's room. I listened but if I did it was only once, so I kept on changing my sheets took everything to the laundromat, returned home made my bed and left the house. The door was still unchanged.

I told Gerald and he said, "Mind yours; remember, Eartha said stay out of her room."

I said, "Yeah, but I'm starting to worry. She usually is in the club some nights, and I haven't seen her in lately."

He said, "Curiosity killed the cat."

I went to bed that night but in the morning I opened Eartha's door. The room had an awful smell I went over to the bed and there lay Eartha all beat up. Her skin was dry she was very weak and she smelled terrible. I got a pan of water and cleaned her up. I put water on her tongue, and changed the bed with her in it. She was so sick I went and found a doctor. Eartha needed more care than I could give. She needed medicine. She definitely had an infection and needed at least a few stitches. JB had beaten her bad on her back with a coat hanger then forced a beer bottle in her vagina until it tore. She was torn to the rectum and bleeding as if she had a baby and ripped the perineum. There went most of my savings. I paid for the doctor and the medicines. After two to three weeks went by, Eartha was getting better and able to walk. I cooked and fed her while she was sick. I liked her she was nice rough but nice. She and I got to be friends. We had long talks. I tried to understand what caused JB to beat her like this. This was when men beat their women all the time as discipline, but not like this. These kind of men beat their women so frequently it was common some women thought the man didn't love them if he wasn't jealous enough to beat them if he thought she was paying some other guy attention.

She said, "You are so green. You need to move out of here because people will think JB has a new woman."

I said, "I don't want your husband."

She said, "JB is not my husband; he's my pimp. I am his number one girl, and I love him. I'm a professional prostitute. Didn't you know?"

I said no. She said, "Didn't you see me in the club?"

I said, "Yeah, but I never saw you with anyone like the others."

She said, "My dates are arranged in advance. Didn't you notice I would leave and return?"

I said, "Yeah, but I made nothing of it."

She shook her head. She said, "Your reputation will go down staying here, you need to leave."

I said, "When I didn't have a place to stay, you let me live here, so screw people. I don't care what they think. I work an honest job for my money, so until they pay my bills and maybe not then, I'll do as I please."

Eartha was walking now and I knew JB the scavenger he was would come back soon. I tried to talk her into another way of making a living. Breath wasted she liked what she did. She said she kept the freaks off the street the clients she catered to wanted weird favors. She said most of them were married, but didn't dare let their spouses know how perverted their sexual desires were. She performed special services at $300 for three minutes or whatever time it took for an egg timer to drain. A golden shower, she peed on them, usually took less than three minutes but still cost $300. She walked on them with high heels and even sat on their face. She said most of these men were not interested in plain sex. They wanted totally freaky sex. Most dates sold at a minimum for at least $900 of which she had about seven a night or day. JB arranged study clients that could afford the service. Most of them were steady weekly clients. He took all the money, bought her food clothes, and things she needed to look and smell good. He kept it all. She kept nothing. Not to judge, but if I had to do this using my tools I certainly would want to keep my money. That's what happened she arranged a private date JB found out and he beat her until she gave him the money. For a mere $200 he beat her like that. Driving a beer bottle in her vagina kept her from working four to five weeks Beating her on the butt with twisted but wrapped clothes hangers kept her from lying on her back. Without money she would have nothing. No food, no anything and have to beg him for help. Pimps did their women that way to make them dependent on them. They never marred the girls faces, but they whipped the girls' bodies often and deprived them of food for any disobedience. This time I was there, so Eartha didn't have to beg. I knew like clockwork after a week or two JB would be back soon as he thought she was able to turn a dollar. He wouldn't care if she was well or not. She was just a cash cow to him. I asked her why she did this. Why do you allow this? She said she loved JB. He was the only one she had real sex with for her own pleasure. Eartha was a woman currently married to a well-known football player who she said loved her. Who was playing for a major NFL team. It was hard for me to understand the reason she would leave a life like that with him for a life like this. JB wasn't even cute. I just stared at her. This life was definitely not one anyone should want, but there she lay still recovering from being very beat up and still in love with that little short, butt hole who did it. I still do not understand how making her use her body, taking the money she earned by having to have sex with some pervert yielding to his or her ideas of sexual pleasure, beating her senseless and using her when and however he pleased made her love him. I just don't get it. Maybe Eartha was right maybe I was green, and if then still cause I'm older, more experienced with life it's crazy turns and people and I still don't get it. In fact, he would have feared ever sleeping anywhere near me and definitely not with me again in this life or the next. Just the thought of the consequence would have put fear in his heart and brought shivers to his spine. As predicted JB was back smiling and carrying on as if nothing had happened. Eartha was her old self elegant, smiling, obedient and quiet.

I was still cooking, working and saving for my own house. I wanted to have enough money to go to school and go get my child. My vision was we move to a nice place where my baby could play in her own yard with other kids. Where I was living was ruff for me and certainly was no place to bring a child.

A few months went by and one morning while it was still dark Eartha came blasting into my room quickly followed by JB. Before I could say, "What the?" JB fired a sawed off over my head which took out half the wall. Then he calmly walked out. Dry wall was everywhere. Eartha and I were covered in plaster. Briko blocks were in the wall, so they stopped the bullet from traveling into another wall or the kitchen fortunately.

I said to Eartha, "I'm leaving. You can come with me. He won't act that way if you are in my house. One day he's going to kill you and I'll be darned if he takes me out, too."

In the next few days, I went looking for a place to live. At the same time, I was accepted to LPN school in Nashville. I figured I wouldn't be at their house much, it was cheaper to stay. Finding a place would cost more than I could afford after the Eartha doctor expense. What with class in the day time and working at night I would rarely see them, so I didn't move.

After a very strange interview with the administrator of the LPN program who asked if I took birth control and told me not to have babies or get married for the duration of the program, all to which I agreed. I admit I had some special help answering the questions from one of the instructors shaking her head yes behind the administrator as she questioned me. With her help I finally was approved to be seated in the class. That was a day long coming one I will never forget. I sat in the front row about three seats from the door and two away from the desk. I closed my eyes and talking to myself, I thanked my mom for the strength she instilled in me by example and said this is for your mom and promised her I would do well.

I rode the Greyhound bus every day to Nashville and every evening back to Clarksville. I had to go early but it was not too bad I slept on the bus coming and going and did some homework when I could. The teacher made the class fun. She called me to her desk one day and said you know this class is for Davidson County residents only. You can't live in another county and attend here, word to the wise. Oh my, I thought I live in Clarksville Montgomery County, and she knows. I wasn't dropping out and I wasn't getting put out. I had no money for an apartment and just enough to ride the bus and eat every day. For one night I decided to try to sleep under the bridge on Charlotte Avenue. It was dry and close to school. I could walk. I thought I could save a few nights' bus fare by sleeping there. I tried it. One night was enough. It was dark, smelly, scary and very dirty. After class the next day I washed my uniform in the sink in the bathroom then I put it on the radiator to dry. As I waited for the uniform to dry I got on the bed with Resusci Annie and fell asleep. Missed my bus.

Too late to venture to the bridge, so I slept there. When I woke I thought about it. If I stay here I'll have no job. If I leave I'll get kicked out of school. I had very little money left, so I figured I needed to live free until I could find work in Nashville. If I had to could get here early and wash up I could stay late and wash my clothes and dry them on the radiators. I figured I can do anything I need to do to stay in school. I'll sleep under the bridge. For about two days I slept under the bridge. It was still scary, dirty and smelly not to mention the area where I slept was rocky. As I lay awake one night cold, it came to me that Resusci Annie was sleeping in the lab on a bed. She is not alive. I'm human on the ground and she has a bed. This made no sense she was a doll and I was human. I needed to be in her bed. The next day after class I waited until everyone left, washed my uniforms in a bathroom, washed me, and waited on the janitor to finish in the class room. As soon as he cut off the light and left me and my few belongings moved in. I hid my things in an unused broom closet, Resusci Annie went to the floor and I got in her bed. I slept like a baby. No pea smell, no rocks, no dirt floor, and there was quiet. No traffic. It was quiet here, too, but this quiet was good, not scary. I left the blind open, so at first light about 5:00 A.M. I would wake up. A great night. I got up made the bed put Annie back on her bed, smoothed out my uniform, got dressed went to the bathroom washed up brushed my teeth, hid my stuff and went to the corner restaurant for breakfast. By the time the class came in at 8:00 A.M. I was arriving, too.

This went on for about three weeks until one night a janitor caught me asleep and turned me into Mrs. Lasaine, one of the instructors. She was a, very stanch lady sort of like a reverend mother in a nunnery. She called me to her office. I thought I'm out she is going to throw me out.

She said, "Why are you sleeping here?"

I said, "I want to stay in class and if I had stayed in Clarksville I'd be put out of this class and I can't let that happen this is my one chance. I can't afford an apartment. I can barely afford to eat. I gave up my place in Clarksville, so here I am. I need a job."

She said, "You need a place to live."

I said, "Yes, I do."

She said, "Let's see what I can do."

She called the manager at JC Napier projects and spoke with him about an apartment. He said he had one not cleaned up yet she said she'll take it. She told me to go see him. The janitor drove me over there. The rent was according to income, so I think I was to pay about $20 a month. I'm sure Mrs. Lasaine paid the first month. I didn't. I was so excited, so grateful. When the manager showed me around I was jumping up and down inside. To me this was a palace. My very own palace. The apartment had a big heater in the living room and hot and cold water in the kitchen. Upstairs it had a bathroom with a tub. It was mine I didn't have to share it with a neighbor or anyone and no man helped me get it. I thought I would cry I was so happy. It was missing furniture and curtains but it was mine.

After a few days, I went to the hospital morgue and asked for morgue sheets. I stitched them gently into plastic drapes. I used the neck and foot ties as tiebacks. I went to Stretches furniture store down town Nashville and told them my husband was in Vietnam, which was not a lie, and got enough credit for a couch, two mattresses and a kitchen table set. I got two beds and two dressers from the Goodwill painted them and I was all set. I wrote Billy my new address and in about two months my child support checks began to come. Life got easier. I went home to Pittsburgh and got my daughter. My Mom and her had grown close in my absence, so I hated to make her leave but I did. I asked my mom to come with us, but she said no Pittsburgh was her home.

Things were good. Dalise was off to school in the morning and I was off to classes. She walked with other kids and I took the bus. I got friendly with the bus driver on that route enough to invited him to dinner after that I was riding free with a pocket full of tokens.

It was Easter afternoon. Dalise and I were on the corner near our apartment waiting on the bus. We were invited to my girlfriend's home for dinner. The bus must have just passed when we got there because we stood waiting about thirty minutes. As we waited this nice car pulls up to the curve and the man said the bus doesn't run regular on holidays want a ride. This was an age when people offered strangers rides and people excepted without too much fear. We had been standing a long while and I wanted to get to my friend's home before dinner was served, so I said yes. There was a well-dressed, dark complected man in the car and he spoke in a deep clear soft voice.

He said, "You and your sister should not get in cars with strange men; you could get hurt."

I pulled my gun out of my pocket and said, "A strange man could get hurt."

He said, "Woo, little girl!"

I said, "I'm not a little girl."

I knew I looked way younger than I was. Always had. I had long thin red braids hanging over my shoulders with bows at the ends. I remember Billy my first and second husband saying I'm not taking your clothes to the cleaners anymore they think I'm living with a child. I weighed about eighty pounds fully dressed if that and I was four feet eleven inches tall. I got in movies paying a child fare. Most folks said I looked about fourteen years old. I never got upset about that because I figured my youthful look was bound to be a look that would be useful in the future.

Frank said, "I was just trying to tell you, I'm okay, but you should not hop in cars with strangers it's very dangerous."

I said, "I know; that's why I carry a gun."

He asked, "Where are you going?"

I said, "Monroe Street. We were invited to eat dinner with friends."

As we drove and talked Frank began to realized I just looked like a child, but was far from one. As I think about it I don't think I was ever a child. As long as I can remember there were always grown-up things on my mind. Dolls were too expensive and I had nowhere to play with them anyway.

Frank asked, "How are you getting home?"

I said, "The bus."

He said, "I'll come get you if you promise not to shoot me."

I replied, "It's okay. I'm use to the bus don't want you to cut short or miss your dinner for me."

He said, "No, I want to. I'm not missing anything; I'm enjoying you."

I said, "Okay, thanks, that would be nice."

He asked "What time?"

I said, "About seven."

The day was good we had a good dinner, and lots of fun, but it was mostly with strangers. I missed my mom and our dinners. I worried if she had dinner. I hated that Mom was alone. I thought next holiday I'd send for her and we will all have dinner together here. Even with that emptiness it was a good day. Frank came as promised and took us home. Well only to the corner from where he picked me up. I was over showing strange men where I lived. I had a bad incident before, so no more. In our conversation I revealed that I caught the 7:30 A.M. bus on the same corner each morning to go to school. Frank said he went to work that way every morning and could pick me up and drop me at school if I wanted. I said, "Yeah, that would be great!"

Next morning I was on the corner waiting on the bus just in case and along came Frank. Looks like I had a permanent ride no more bus, no more being nice to sleazy bus drivers to get free token. Cant label them all. Some of the guys were genuinely nice especially one driver. He got a new route then I got this other one. I had him over for dinner to say thanks. Thought he was nice like the other one. He seemed nice at first two or three months, but after dinner that night he got creepy. He tried to hug me. I refused and pulled away. He asked where the bathroom was I pointed upstairs. He went up the stairs, but he stayed up there so long I came up to see where he was. He was in my bed. My daughter was home in her room asleep across the hall, so I quietly tried to get him out, but when I pulled him he pulled me, ripped my top and bra, ripped my underwear by the seat we fought but he was two hundred-plus pounds and way bigger than me. I didn't want my child to wake and see this, so I was unable to stop the attempted rape until I wiggled to the end of the bed where my gun was. I was able to grip and cock it at his head. I said, "Get up and get out or I'll have you carried out in sections." He reached for his clothes. I kicked them to him and said, "Dress outside." I backed him down the steps to the front door and put him out naked. I was so scared I knew if he lunged at me I would have shot him. I didn't want to do that but I didn't want him to hurt me and definitely did not want my child to wake up to me killing him. He never came back.

I still rode the bus until I met Frank. I missed the bus if I saw him driving. No I didn't turn him in no one would believe that nice guy with the big smile invited to a home for dinner would try to rape the host. Back then such a thing would have been hard to prove and killing him not worth it the consequences too expensive and too time consuming. This was a new and important day. Frank and I became friends. He asked where I worked I told him I was a student had to give up my job as a waitress in a club in Clarksville when I moved here. I told him I depended on child support for now. I'm trying to find work. My teacher is trying to get me a job with one of the doctors at the medical school, but as yet, nada.

About six months later, I found out Billy had come home on leave and gotten married. I think I got one child support check from him after that. When we separated this time Billy sent Dalise checks himself. The military probably didn't know we were divorced. Billy always sent his check on time. Never missed till now. Three months went by no check I thought he had been deployed and the check had been delayed in route. I tried calling him at his home no answer. Six months went by still no check. Reluctantly, I called Billy's job and got him. I hated to do that cause the military frowns on soldiers who shirk their bills and especially child support. That soldier finds themselves in deep trouble if their CO finds out. I said we are struggling here no money. I asked him why no checks? He said what do you mean no checks.

I said, "I haven't gotten any check or money from you for over six months."

He said, "Well, I sent it."

I said, "I'll check the post office; maybe there's a glitch there."

In the meantime, I became so sick I couldn't get out of bed. I had no money to go to the doctor and no one to take care of Dalise if I were kept in the hospital, so there I lay sweaty, coughing, hot then cold sick.

I think three or four days must have gone by when my daughter ran upstairs and said, "There's a man at the door asking for you. He said tell you he's Frank."

I looked up and Frank was standing behind her. He said, "You look terrible. You been like this since I saw you?"

I said, "Yeah. I'm so sick. I missed school, too."

He picked me up covers and all and down the steps he carried me. We're going to the doctor now. He carefully poured me into the back seat of his car and put Dalise in the back beside me. It was embarrassing. I looked like slop and probable did not smell good. I washed up a little but had not bathed in days. Hadn't been able to bath I was too weak to stand. I just washed up with Dalise's help.

The emergency room doctor said I had pneumonia. I probably would have died if not for Frank. Frank paid the ER bill, got my medicine bought food, cooked it and helped me bath, and stayed all day to take care of me. He was amazing. Thursday, Friday, Saturday and Sunday he only left at night and was back by morning.

By Monday I was able to go back to school. I wasn't 100 percent but couldn't miss anymore class and still be in school. Frank drove me to the door. I mean literally to the door. I thought he was going to climb the three steps at the school with the car. After class he picked me up. He cooked and took care of the laundry. Dalise and he even did her homework. Dalise was the leg man running up and down the stairs with messages and food. Me I did nothing just rested in bed.

In another week I was up and running. I don't think Frank slept while I was sick. He cared for me all day and left only to shop for food and about 10:00 P.M. each night he was gone till morning. Frank said he had an event he wanted me to attend with him. Mind now he was twenty-two years older than me, so I was leery cause I knew his friends would think I was some young pick up after his money. Frank was not a love interest for me we were just friends with great benefits. He and I were good for each other. Frank was extremely nice to me, but I knew he had another side. He had to have cause everywhere he went except at my house he had a guy with him who he called his buddy but seemed to me to be his body guard. I noticed men and women were careful how they talked to him. Gabby, his friend, body guard, did not let many people get in touching range of him unless Frank nodded okay except me. I could do anything to Frank and he just smiled and his guys shook their head.

This night Frank must have wanted his friends or some women to see me, so he took me to a hairdresser had my hair done and bought me new clothes. By 8:00 P.M., I had a babysitter and I was very dressed up. He picked me up and we went to a night club. We danced and had a great time he drank Johnnie Walker Red and I drank coke with a cherry. I still don't know who he impressed we just seem to have fun. He never left me for a minute. Walked me to the bathroom and waited at the entrance. I did not sleep at my house that night he had to go to work, so we went to his apartment for him to change about midnight. It was raining so bad I got soaked on the way in. I took of my clothes off got in his bed to warm up. Seeing me in his bed he got in, too. For an older man he was still able, very warm and easy. I fell asleep. When I woke Frank was gone. He came back in the morning. We slept an hour or two more then he got dressed took me home picked up the sitter and left.

Never seeing him go into a specific work place I wondered where he worked. He always wore a suit, white shirt, no tie, black hat and very nice shoes. Frank always looked creased.

I asked him, "Where do you work?"

He said, "I'm retired."

I asked, "Retired from what?"

He got quiet. Then he said, the Army; I retired after two years. I haven't had a job since. I'm a professional gambler."

I said, "Oh."

He said, "That's all, oh."

I said, "Yeah. How do you get money to gamble if you do not work?"

He replied, "A working man should not gamble. They have too much to lose. How would you like to work for me?"

I said, "Doing what? I can't play cards."

He smiled and said, "As my banker."

"I don't have any money. How can I be your banker?"

He laughed and said, "You would carry my money and bring it to me as I needed it."

"Bring it as you need it; that's all! Can I spend any?" I teased.

He said, "If you need it."

"How much can I spend?"

He said, "Whatever you need; just tell me how much you spend and when you spent it."

I said, "Sure. I can't ride the bus and bring you money can I and where would I need to bring it?" I thought he was teasing me. So I played along.

He said, "No, I'll give you my car."

I said, Then what will you drive to the job you said you had and don't?"

He smiled and said, "I'll manage." Turns out he was serious. He gave me his keys and said, "You and the baby need this to get around anyway in a safer manner and I can't always be there." So just like that I had a new car. That evening he gave me somewhere around $30,000. I'd never seen or held so much money. On an average day I carried $35,000-$40,000 in my purse or on my person. I never left the money anywhere it stayed on me in my pocket, purse or pinned securely to my underwear even when I slept. No one but Frank and I knew I carried that money on me every day to school to the bathroom everywhere. When he needed money, he would sometimes send his son to find me and his son would say, "Dad wants you." He would give me a note and leave. He'd say he said you know where he is. The amount would be written down in an envelope. I never gave Frank's money to anyone to deliver. Not even his son. Frank said no one else could deliver his money or ever drive my car. Absolutely no one. Even if Gabby his body guard came after me I still had to go in my car and not send his money. I still carried my gun in fact now I had two one under the seat and one in my pocket. When I went to the gambling house the guard would search me, someone would follow me in, but no one ever took my gun. Frank's body guard would escort me to him. I had to remove my glasses, so the guys couldn't read his cards in them. I never spoke to Frank. I just counted the money to him and left it laying out on the table and left. This was easy. On nights when he won I would just roll in the money, but when he lost I was devastated. I got to feeling possessive like it was my money he was losing. Sometimes it was $10,000, sometimes $20,000-$30,000. I used to freak out at that amount. I'd say how will we get this back. He'd say it's okay don't worry. Sure enough he would make it back. I had money to pay bills and buy stuff and a beautiful new car. I also had twenty-five phones in my name at an address at which I didn't live that I didn't find out about until way later after I left Nashville. If I spent any money, I'd tell Frank. He'd look at me and say okay. I asked him once I said you don't write anything down, how do you keep up with what I have, what I spend and what you lose? He said, "I'm good at math." He was good, very good. He was so accurate he could have been an excellent accountant. He could total in his head a long set of numbers faster than I could with a pencil. He was very smart. He knew to the penny how much I had and what I spent. He could even tell me the day I spent it weeks later. I've always liked to shop, so me with a pocket full of money was dangerous. Frank liked me to look nice all the time, so he never fussed at me for buying clothes.

On one occasion, I went shoe shopping with Frank. It was about noon at 1:00 P.M. I was still at an exclusive store deciding on one pair of shoes out of thirteen pairs.

Quietly he whispered to me, "I have to be at work at two; pick a pair."

I said, "I just can't decide. Which one do you like? They are all so cute."

He looked at the sales lady and said, "We'll take them all."

I said, "All Frank, there's thirteen pairs of shoes here."

He said, "I can count. Pick the one you want at home and return the others; I gotta go."

He shelled out over $1,400, plus tax, at once and this was at sale price. Guess which ones I returned? Right, none. He never said a word. That was Frank he always wanted me to have anything I wanted. I became so spoiled. My dog even had a rhinestone collar because he said the one I bought was for my elephant. Frank was not demanding never wanted much. He enjoyed showing me off like a trinket. Never even raised his voice at me. He just shook his head when he thought I was being stupid. Frank was an all over gentleman.

I was lying in the back seat of his car one day like always when Frank was on a mission, so as not to interfere with anything. Usually I was asleep but this time I was not asleep. I heard one of his friends say you know she is after your money. Why are you fooling around with her anyway, she is a little girl? Frank said, "I like nice shirts. I have them custom made and delivered. They cost a lot. I don't mind paying for the things I like. I don't like much, her I like and that's no little girl. She could sit on a polar bear's knee and freeze him." That put a quick end to that conversation. If Frank was anything he was direct.

On the way home Frank said, "You know if you were not so honest you would make a hell of a crook."

I said "Why?"

He said, "You are so cold, nothing stirs you."

I smiled. I thought to myself things stir me, but no one will know what, cause if people find out what bothers you it will cause some to use it against you. Frank loved me I'm sure. He would protect me with his life his friends and associates came to know that. Frank knew on my part our relationship was a convenience much like a couple married thirty to forty years who coexist and exchange kindnesses, but no fire, no passion. Frank was sweet to me and I was just as sweet right back day to day we lived, had fun there was no reason to pretend emotion. He knew. Once he mentioned marriage and I immediately said no. He said, "I'll pay your way to college and all through grad school and then when I am unable to do this you can care for me." Frank was forty-four and I was twenty-two—no way. When I would have been forty-four he would be sixty-six. It did occur to me he did need a wife to care for him in his later years, so I thought I need to move out of his way. I knew I would never marry Frank. I was grateful to him for the support he gave me and I cared a lot about him. I wanted him to have a full and good life just not with me. I also knew there was a side of Frank I had never met. That side popped out once when he and I were walking from the Top Hat, a club across from my apartment. A women came out of nowhere and grabbed him and started yelling loud and fast and being real ugly to him. He excused himself and said good night to me and asked his body guard to walk me across the street to my apartment. Once we were out of sight across the street I heard a loud slap sound and no more. I asked Gabby should he go back it got mighty quiet Frank may need you?

He said, "Frank wanted me to see you home safely; he'll be all right he's a big boy and he has other friends to help if he needs it. Don't know for sure who got slapped, but I'm pretty sure it wasn't Frank." He came over about an hour later looking every bit as dapper as he was when I saw him last. Not a hair out of place, no marks or bruises I could see.

He said, "You okay?"

I said, "Yes, are you?"

He said, Oh, yeah, sorry for the fuss. Just checking on you. I'll see you soon, gotta go to work."

He left and I went to bed because it was about midnight. Frank was always sweet to me never raised his voice. I credit him with saving my life and doing the most to help me get through school. We remained friends but I began seeing other people. I wanted Frank to have a full life with someone who loved him. He deserved that.

At long last I graduated from LPN school. My mom came down to see me. Billy had shipped all of my furniture from the trailer to my mom's house in Pittsburgh. While Mom was visiting me for graduation someone broke in and stole all of it. I was devastated. Mom was so proud of me she told all her neighbors where she was going and when she was leaving. This was a mistake. It's a recipe for getting robbed in the city. Ce la vie.

Fate plays tricks. Now that I was settled and doing well Donnie called and wanted me to come to Ohio. Even though it had been so long and I'd been through so much trying to survive I was excited. Remembering what Donnie and I had I was willing to go see if it was still there. None of the relationships I had ever compared to what Donnie and I shared, and I never got over him. Donnie was still the one. I explained to Frank my dilemma how I had to go see. He understood. I packed and left. I still loved Donnie it's just that sometimes situations make things difficult and people do what they need to do to keep pace with life. My first stop was Pittsburgh. I went home to see my mom first and to leave my daughter with her. I caught the bus to Cleveland Ohio. Donnie met me at the bus station. I was taken back by his look, it was different his hair was longer but he was just as sweet.

We got to my motel and it was as if we were never apart. We made love from the door to the bed. We talked for a while about his plan for our future. He wanted us to get a house. Donnie always had a plan. The one thing I never worried about was what's next. Donnie always took care of that. He still smelled wonderful and his arms felt safe and strong as ever. Nothing had been lost. There was something about him he was so amazing. I don't remember if he called his mother or she called him, but in a flash everything took an about face. Seems his uncle or some relative died and his mom wanted him to drive her to Georgia. He said, okay, so I asked, can I go? He said no this is a bad time. I'll be back in a few days. I knew right then this was not going to work. When Momma calls he runs, which is okay actually good for a man to treat his mother with such regard, but I should have been able to go with him since I traveled this distance to a strange town to be with him. This was our first hour together in a long, long time. That was my way of thinking anyway, but it was not his. So he left me there to drive his momma to Georgia. After he was gone I sat on the bed in this strange motel room hungry cause I hadn't eaten wondering where the stores were. I thought I don't know a soul here. I don't even know where a store is and I'm not sure of the neighborhood. The more I thought the more I felt abandoned and that this was not the place for me. I'm not playing second fiddle to his mom. I knew she didn't like me, so from the beginning it would have been rough. I thought by now he would have gotten a set and explained me to her. I repacked my stuff got a cab and took the bus back to Pittsburgh. That was it never saw or heard from Donnie again. I stayed to visit Mom in Pittsburgh awhile before I returned to Tennessee. My friends were still playing cards on the porch. My dear friend's husband had just released from jail again.. Looking at the neighbors' children, they looked just like my friend's daughters. Nothing had changed. I was not missing a thing. No one was going anywhere. Don't think they cared to. I was better off in Tennessee. That out of my system I was fine. Somehow the past always gets remembered fonder than the present. Frank was not the love of my life, but he was a darn nice guy. I could count on him.

I came home to Tennessee and got a job working at a local hospital. I graduated and was now I was an LPN. While working in the hospital I met a dental student named Michael. Mike, as he wanted to be called, and I went around for a while. I liked him. He was going somewhere. I admired that, but I feared him. The problem with the Medical or dental students is after you devote and support them four or five years at graduation the wife, kids and dog show up and you're out on your butt. Almost at the same time I was seeing Mike I met Jenell, a recent graduate of mortuary school. A girlfriend and I were in a club and along came Jenell. Uninvited he pulled up a chair anyway and sat at our table. Handsome my, he looked like Billy Dee. Dressed to perfection and money seemed no object. I didn't drink, so there's only so many sodas I can hold but my girlfriend wow. I thought he would go broke before she stopped ordering on his tab. By the end of the night she was plastered and Jenell was two sips shy of passing out. Marion was in no shape to drive and I drove with her. Jenell was just as bad his head was at least off the table. I wouldn't have ridden with either of them driving anyway. I had no car, so what a pickle. I needed a cab. Jenell said I'll take you home. It's my birthday and I have a new car outside bought it today. I said no thanks. He asked can you drive a stick? I said it's been awhile but I'm willing to try if that's all we got. This was a very small expensive sports car an Austin Healy. I could see the dents I might put in it just leaving the parking lot. Somehow I managed to get out without hitting anything and we all fit in this little car and I was driving. I dropped Marion off first and then I realized this guy lived in Clarksville. I was not about to drive him home; besides, how would I get back? So I took him home with me. Almost dragged him in the door. Put him on the sofa downstairs and went upstairs to bed. In the morning I guess he figured out he was in a strange place and went searching for his wallet which had fallen from his pocket to the floor when I laid him on the sofa. As I came down stairs he asked where's my wallet? I said under the sofa where you slept. He said I thought it was lost. I said, "No, it fell out your pocket." I know he thought I took it, but he never said it. He knew that would have happened if he had passed out and no one looked out for him in instances and most places. I didn't know what else to say, so I asked, "Want breakfast?"

He said, "No, I've got to get to work."

I said, "Okay."

Then he turned in the doorway and asked, "Can I buy you dinner this evening?" I said sure.

He said, "I'll be back about seven," as he fumbled for his keys.

I said, "Your keys, I still have them; I'm sorry."

I thought he had spent his entire paycheck last night, because he spent well over $500, but he was now wanting to spend more. Seven came, and so did he. We went for dinner and dancing. It was Saturday night, we had a ball, in Nashville in those days, fun was on every corner. The night ended with an I'll call you. I said fine. I wasn't sure I made enough of an impression for him to want to call. He hopped in his car and off he went. I thought I'll never see him again but I did. Monday after work there he stood.

I said, "I have a car," and he said, "Ride with me." It was eleven o'clock, a nice night, he was beautiful to look at a Billy Dee kind of handsome and I really didn't want to go home. Frank had not called for money and Mike was studying for exams. I was free for a while. Jenell and I rode around down town talking. We had a snack at Popeye's and he took me back to my car. He moved in to kiss me, but I moved away and turned my cheek.

He said, "I'm sorry." I got out of his car and into mine. After that he showed up almost every night as I was leaving the building. I asked why are you so interested in me surely with your money and looks there must be plenty women you could have and not drive so far to get. He lived about an hour's drive from me.

He said, "You're right, but I want you and you don't live where I live."

I said, "No, you don't I have way too much baggage." He smiled. What a smile all dimples and his dentist must have been proud. He had glistening white straight teeth.

He said, "I used to watch you when you lived in Clarksville."

I said, "I don't remember seeing you. Where were you?"

He said, "I lived next door to Eartha."

I said, "Oh—why didn't you speak?"

He said, "I don't know guess because I thought you were a hooker."

I said, "Guess everyone in Clarksville does."

He said, "Yeah, I'm sure they do. You didn't make many friends."

I said, "I worked at night and some during the day I was too busy to make friends."

He said, "So you hung out with Eartha?"

I said, "Yeah, she was nice. She did what she did and I did what I did—no judgment. I said I'm not a hooker, I didn't need money then and don't need money now trust me I'm very, very okay. I don't know what you're thinking or what your intensions are, but I can assure you your money can't buy you anything here. I don't think we should see each other if that's what you think."

He said, "I don't want anything except to spend time with you, get to know you and you get to know me that's all. The past is the past."

After that we never talked about yesterday. One afternoon we were at the back door of my apartment when Frank came to the front but had no key, so he was knocking. I let him knock cause the situation was awkward. Jenell said if that were me at the door when I did get in

I'd kick your tail. I thought he was just being sympathetic with Frank, so I ignored his words. Hind sight is twenty-twenty a lesson learned if a person makes a comment like that with no reservation it would be wise to hear them well and take heed. Jenell told me he was an Elk and had some big title. They were having their annual ball near Memphis in Humboldt and asked me to go with him. I said yes. It was a chance to wear a long gown dress up and to meet some of his friends. I wore a green long gown and he wore a black tuxedo everyone commented on how we made an amazing couple. Jenell outwardly was a striking figure. Smooth skin and curly black hair quite handsome. There were Morticians, bankers, big wigs of wall sort there. All of these people, including Jenell drank heavily. He was busy glad handing everyone and left me alone at the table hours. I was not happy. One hour in and I was ready to leave. Three hours and somewhere like four drinks more he was red eyed, still smiling and shaking hands when we finally left. I was cold sober. At that time, I still didn't drink, so I was bored to tears and tired. All I wanted to do was get out of my shoes and go to bed. When we got to the hotel room Jenell laid over the bed and pulled out a beautiful engagement ring. this was no regular ring. He had it made. It had a large black carved out rose with gold edge with a large diamond in the center. It has small diamonds sprinkled over the carved rose buds laying on their side left and right of the large rose. It was a one of a kind ring he had made for me. He said I have a problem. My inheritance requires I buy ten houses from my dad at $1,000 each and be married by the time I reach twenty-eight in order to get the money he plans to give me in his will. If I do not comply my sister will get the bigger share and his wife the other. My dad wants to know I'm stable enough to control my life and his money. I have the houses now I need a wife and soon. I married a girl on my lunch hour at the court house because she was pregnant, but had it annulled soon after she and I were awful together. I will support the baby. I said what do you need from me. He said I need you to marry me. I think I can afford your habit. I have enough money to get you out of the projects and you and your daughter would have a house and live well. I said I live here by choice and I do live well. I'm not in love with you. I don't see my advantage. He said if it doesn't work you can leave it's fine. I care for you and I will work to make you happy. I said let me think about it. He said okay. All my friends thought he was a great catch. He was well thought of in the community. Seems reputation is what people think of you and his was good. I should have considered his character more than reputation as my mother use to say all that glitters is not gold. I could say he showed the glitter then I must consider I did not have a gun to my head when I excepted the offer. I saw the glitter. I thought I'm really sick of the projects and I am getting in too deep with Frank. Don't know how much of his business I'm in or needed to be in. Not because of Frank but the folks who backed him. I didn't know them and didn't want to. Guess they were alright cause sometimes Frank would lose $30,000-$40,000 on a week night and $50,000-$60,000 on a Saturday. He'd just go get more -and once again I had $50,000-$60,000 to carry around. Michael was a student and not ready to commit. In fact he once said You want it now I can only do later. Should have waited, but hind sight is twenty-twenty.

One night I saw Michael's underwear were grey, looking dirty. I know now that was probably because he washed his underwear with his jeans, but at the time I thought he was not clean. Bad choice. I married Jenell moved to Clarksville with his firm promise we would move back to Nashville one day. I didn't want to live in Clarksville. We had a beautiful garden wedding. Everyone was dressed so elegantly and I didn't know a single one of those people. I wondered how I got myself in to this mess. My common sense kicked in too late I'd given up my apartment and said goodbye to Frank. On the way down the aisle I didn't even hear the music. I stepped slowly with a strong urge to turn back. Should have. Jenell planned everything even the honeymoon. He told me we were we were going. It was to be spent in New York. We were driving, so we left in the middle of the reception. By that night we reached New Jersey. We were spending the night at his relatives' home in New Jersey, not too far from New York. I realized later we were staying with the relative in Jersey and just visiting New York. okay no Problem. His folks were nice, but this was a honeymoon. I came to be with Jenell and he was not attentive. Of course we did the usual sex thing at night, but he went hunting with the guys early the first day and just left me. He didn't even say I'm leaving. Left early the following morning, too. He was quickly mooring into the butt hole that he permanently remained. I think the third day we did get to drive to New York to see a museum. While we were in the museum the car was towed away. We parked where a lot of drivers was fighting for a space, but as there was a sign on a pole hidden by a tree that we failed to see which said no parking. We came out and a little guy selling hot dogs from a cart was there. Jenell asked where's my car the guy said a little car? We said yes. He said they tow it away. We asked where, why? He said to the pier because you parked under a no parking sign. As we looked closer there it was and it said no parking. We caught a bus to the Pier trying to get the car back. It took all day to retrieve the car and, pay the outrageous fees for towing and a ticket for illegal parking. A lot of people chauffeurs and drivers alike were at the Pier to get their car from a bevy of very short, very rude policemen and women who never looked up to see who they were talking with. When we finally got the car it was wrecked on one side from careless towing. Jenell tried to sue the city of New York for damages but found that to sue New York you had to be a resident of New York. That was my honeymoon day in New York City. Never saw much and didn't buy anything. Back to Jersey we went. I was so disillusioned and it had only been about forty-eight hours. I expected more from him since we had so much fun dating. I figured we'd go on dating and maybe we would grow on each other and this marriage may work. I did not lose sight of the fact that this was not a marriage because of love but for a purpose with an arrangement. Still there should have been and I expected common courtesy. Instead he only got worse. I didn't dare tell any of my old friends how I was being treated or Jenell may have not made it home one night. When I would meet any of them on the street I could only talk to them only if Jenell was not around because he was crazy jealous. He always thought, or said he thought, I was secretly planning a date with the guys and he just didn't want me associating with the trash women, as he called them. He would smile at the person and give them his business card, and say if you ever have a need for a ride or help in anyway just call. All that sweet talk was just to promote his business. Jenell owned a funeral home and wanted their body or the family member's body if they were sick or about to die. He was a mortician a slick one, but a very good one he could restore a body quite well I must admit. He often came to Nashville to help at a funeral home there. After that person walked away if it was a woman he'd say you're my wife I don't want you talking to that trash. If it was a man he'd beat me up when we got home accusing me of flirting or planning a date. He was certifiably crazy.

One winter night very late he came in the door and started chocking and hitting me asking where was he? I was asleep in bed and had no idea what he was talking about. He started ripping the closets apart He thought someone was hiding in there. He was ranting and raving about some must be in the house cause there were footprints outside. When he dragged me to the door I saw that there was deep snow and prints someone was probably looking for an address and walked in their own footprint to our door to see the address then back to their car in their own print, so it appeared that they came but did not leave. He raved and went on till he was tired. He was so mean. Once when I was six months pregnant I was sitting in a Bamboo swivel chair in the living room holding my dog when out of the blue he hit me in the face so hard I landed on the floor and slid a foot away from the chair across the room. This was because I was petting my little dog on my lap. He said put the dog down. He was crazy jealous of everyone and everything even the dog. I figured he just enjoyed beating up on me. I should have left. Don't know why I stayed guess cause by then I was pregnant no money of my own and nowhere to go that I wanted to be. I burned my bridges in Nashville. Frank was sweet to me but I was just in his way. He needed to get on with marrying some-one because he was getting up there in age and he wouldn't move if I came back. Jenell had the advantage. I could have called Frank or Harold, but neither of them would not have been tolerant of Jenell hitting me. Jenell would not have wanted to recon with either of them. He would have required his own services. Didn't want anyone in jail or dead over my stupidity, so I endured. When I lived in the projects I rarely locked my doors a lot of the time cause a group of the locals would play card in my kitchen most every day and leave me money and food. They always left before my daughter got home from school and cleaned up any mess they made. They knew not to tear up or take anything because Frank was highly respected and they knew Frank protected me like I was an egg he had hatched. He always spoke soft to me, but if you knew him you knew not to judge him by his voice. His eyes said it all. A kid was murdered on my step one night or fell there to die. I was asleep and didn't hear anything. I was used to sleep-ing soundly no matter the noise unless it was in my house. The club across the street was always loud and all kind of noise came from the traffic. The next morning a policeman checking out the crime asked if I was aware of the killing and had I seen or heard anything. I said no if I saw anything I would not be talking to you. I'd be dead, too. That was a neighborhood where you saw, or heard no evil. If you did you could come down with an acute case of death. My daughter could take care of herself, too. I often left my daughter home alone one hour at night because I worked three to eleven, and Frank left at ten—no later than 10:30 P.M. The locals knew it and watched my house. My friend Marion lived in eye view of my door and watched it diligently till I got home. Messing with my house would have had serious reper-cussions and everyone knew that. Besides I taught my daughter to shoot a gun at the window if she thought someone was breaking in.

One night I thought I had to work but was not on the schedule, so I returned home. I was locked out this never happened, so I tried to get in through the window and she almost shot me. Bullets whizzed over and crossed my head. I got down and went over to Franks apartment to sleep. Never told her she may have killed her mother. So it wasn't that I couldn't take care of myself it was that I did not want to chance losing my child with a jail sentence. Many was the day I could have fixed the problem with one phone call, but I knew how to wait. Things change if you just wait, take a breath and wait and they did.

The baby was born. She was beautiful coal black locks of hair cute and cuddly. Jenell was thrilled he came home every day at lunch to see the baby. We named her Genae Angela but Jenell called her Peaer. Before Genae was born Jenell came home for lunch because I worked nights and was in bed by then. He'd wake me up just to have sex. No not love it was far removed from that. I can't be amorous with someone who beats the heck out of me whenever they want for no reason.

Genae started to have dark stools and cry a painful cry more and more and for long periods of time. I took her to the doctor two or three times to have her checked for this. but he said the black was from the iron in the Enfamil and the crying was just her altered sleep pattern. Still I asked Jenell could we get a second opinion in Nashville maybe at Vanderbilt. He said no. These were good doctors they knew what they were doing it would be an insult to them to ask for a second opinion. They had treated him and his sister for years.

An insurance agent came to the door to see if I wanted insurance on the baby. I said no we will do it later. I was not working and didn't want to ask Jenell for the premiums. I went back to work soon after that and thought about getting the insurance. It was too late. In about a week after I turned the insurance down I looked at the baby and she had blue spots on her. I rushed her to the emergency room and they admitted her. We got to the room and Genae stopped breathing. Jenell wanted her transported to Vanderbilt Hospital in Nashville. Now he was concerned, Genae was throwing blood clots and so now he was concerned. Not when it could have helped but now. As I stood over her bed she was so little and so sick. As I stared at her she stopped breathing, I began CPR and screamed for help, and a suction machine she seemed to be throwing up. The nurses from ICU came running, but was reluctant to touch my baby because she was pregnant. She explained she didn't want to get too close cause she was not sure what my baby had the labs were not back. She feared for her pregnancy. I noticed all the hesitation but she did rush the baby to ICU. It wasn't long after the transfer we were told they were transporting my baby to Vanderbilt. More intense care then this hospital could provide was needed. Genae was throwing blood clots. The ambulance came she was loaded on, Jenell and I followed in our car. Jenell and I had little to say going up the interstate we rode frightened quietly behind the ambulance. I was so scared, I knew how bad Genae looked and I had just brought her back with CPR. Jenell was scared, too. I could tell he was now ready to do anything to keep his baby alive. I thought now you care, I begged you to let me take her to Nashville for a second opinion and you said no. On arrival at Vanderbilt we were taken to a waiting area. In a matter of minutes, a doctor came in and said, "I'm sorry your baby died in the ambulance on the way to the hospital. She had DIC (disseminated intravascular coagulation), a large word for moving blood clots. He asked if they could have permission to perform an autopsy. We said, "no because what would that do she was gone and knowing the cause would not bring her back." We later agreed after the doctor explained that it was important to know what caused this in order to avoid the same problem with future children. I did not want this ever to happen again. and I really thought I had brought some germ home from the hospital that caused this. We were told later the cause was hepatitis. Jenell and I were given vaccine by injection because we had hepatitis, too. I really felt guilty thinking I brought this disease home from the hospital. It was twenty-five years later that a friend of mine asked if I knew Jenell was an addict. I replied no. I said he was an alcoholic when I met him but he stopped drinking. She said but he started horse. She named his contact who was now dead. I thought that explained a lot. The mood swings and the anger and anxiety then the calm. He was a functioning drug addict. It was then I realized he was the culprit he had hepatitis from shooting up. He gave it to me during sex and it passed to the baby or maybe the sperm were already infected. I lived in torment for all these years thinking I caused my baby to die and all the while it was Jenell, needles and drugs. The knowledge eased my heart a little to know it was not my careless hand washing that killed my child, but still it was my fault for not selecting more carefully a husband and sex partner. I did not know Jenell was using drugs. I saw no tracks or needle marks. If I had known he was on drugs, that would have been a deal breaker. An addict is dangerous. Out of bed drugs make them crazy and in the bed their diseased and crazy. Jenell should have told me. A person should have a choice to stay with or not stay with a drug user if are told about it, I was not told and look what happened. Jenell began to drink again. He was so depressed and I was little help to him because I was depressed, too. On top of that I blamed him for not allowing me to seek a second opinion which may have saved her. This marriage was wrong in so many ways. I should have left him before and certainly after the honeymoon.

Jenell sold some of his properties to Austin Peay for a tidy sum. With the money he built a small but nice night club. He spent a lot of his time there working the bar. He wouldn't let me help but wanted me there on a bar stool every night. Sitting on a bar stool appearing to be alone is bait for a man to want to talk to you. In a soldier town where the working girls usually sat at the bar alone it was an open invitation. I tried to explain this to Jenell but he said you're with me, so it's okay. Well it wasn't okay cause these guys did not know him or me and when they saw a red headed tiny, well built, well dressed lady at the bar seemingly alone over they came. It was always a problem because Jenell would accuse me of inviting them and planning a meeting, which I didn't but should have because I got the beating later anyway. I needed a way out. I was tired of everything especially trying to please. I just needed money.

On New Year's Eve, I cut my hand on his razor I brought him at the club that night. He sent me home to wait on him to get someone in to take over for him at the bar, so he could take me to get stitches he never came. I called the cops because I thought he was in trouble. The police found him and brought him home the next afternoon. I thought he had gotten mugged for the money from the club recites and was laying somewhere hurt or dead. Jenell once told me about his father being attacked and robbed in his own gauge as he arrived home. Jenell found him just in time. But no this time Mr. Jenell was fine just out partying all night didn't care I was cut needed stitches and bleeding. That morning he had flowers delivered to me at the house. I was certain this man was nuts. Maybe he thought I had bled to death and the flowers were really meant for the funeral. I was living in a situation that was very similar to what my mom had. The time had long passed for me to leave. The dim light in my brain came on full blast. I woke up. It became a matter of where and when to go. Didn't want to return to Pittsburgh again, but I was sure I had to leave here.

A month later Genae my sister-in-law Jenell's twin asked me to go shopping with her in Nashville. I was sure he wouldn't mind since this was his sister. I was glad to get away for the day, so I went and had a good day. I really had a good time. I didn't get to go out much and I had no friends. Jenell was so jealous and disliked everyone. Leaving a store, I met Larry an old friend who had just returned from Vietnam. He and I used to work together on a psychiatric ward on my last job. When I met him on the ward he was so quiet I thought he was a patient. He liked classical music and so did I, especially Camelot, so we got along fine. For a couple of weeks prior to this meeting I had looked out my living room window and from time to time thought I'd seen a man sitting on a large rock at the end of the street near my house. He looked like Larry, but I thought no that's not possible. He's

in Vietnam. As Larry and I talked he revealed he had been sitting outside my house. I asked why. He said I heard that you were being mistreated and he said he was there in hope of helping me. Like how I
asked. He said well let's say I was going to give your husband a man
to hit. A dangerous situation. I worked with Larry and he and I got
very close. As a matter of fact, in Vietnam he became real depressed
after a number of his fellow soldiers were killed. His CO wrote me to
urge me to write him. I wondered how did he get my address. He
wrote Larry has you as his beneficiary. I was shocked. I really didn't
understand that we were not that kind of close not engaged or anything. I did begin to write and asked the CO to ask Larry not to write
back because it would not be good for me. So when he got back he
came and sat on the rock every Saturday to watch my house. Never
came in or knocked. He said if there is anything I can do or you need
anything let me know and gave me his address. When Genae drove
me home that night I walked into a living room full of broken Glass.
Jenell was shooting Johnny Walker Red bottles full of liquor from our
supply of liquor for our club off the piano. When I walked in he
turned to me with the loaded gun and said where were you? I said
your sister asked me to go to Nashville to shop with her. He said you
did not ask me! I said no. I didn't know I had to she is your sister. He
put the gun down and said I have to go pick up the receipts at the club
well discuss this when I get back. I went and undressed and put on
my night gown and slippers. Then a thought came to me he's going
to kill you tonight. I became frightened. He rounded the corner leaving for the club and I figured it was time to go. I thought he has really
gone crazy bullet holes in the wall glass and scotch in every corner of
the room When he gets back he'd probably beat me again or shoot
me. I grabbed my uniforms and shoes, my dog picked up my daughter
from her bed quickly threw all of the stuff in the back seat and her in
the front. I jumped in and drove like a mad man as fast as possible
trying to put distance between me and that place. I made it almost to
the interstate when I looked in my rearview mirror there was Jenell

coming fast behind me. We got to a split in the road and he blocked my car, got out and began walking toward my car. He said let's talk. I yelled stay back no go away. He kept coming I pulled around him barely missing a guard rail. He got back in his car and began to chase me again. There was a bottleneck about two miles up and he pulled his car across most of it leaving room for him to walk. He said let's talk I saw him with that rifle. I said no move your car. If I pulled out, I'd either hit him or his car there was very little road open. I said don't walk any closer but he kept coming. I screamed please move! I got so scared I hit the accelerator, he jumped to one side and I pulled pass him. I felt a thump on the side of my car as I pulled past him and noticed him flying to the right. I kept going. I was so scared. I was sure he would have killed me if he had gotten any closer. Jenell hunted crows often and was a good shot. He could hit a crow at a distance way up in a tree. I was sure if I sat still long enough and he could aim he could shoot me.

I don't know how I made it. I was so shaken. It was raining and I don't see well in the dark. Luckily there was an eighteen-wheeler in front of me I followed it all the way into Nashville. I just couldn't find Larry's street or apartment. It was getting light and still I was wondering around. I was afraid I'd have to return to Clarksville. I got out the car at the Spur gas station across from NES down town and went in to talk with the clerk. I forgot I had on a very sheer see through night gown. The man just stared at me. I realized what he was looking at, so I said this is all I have for now. I had to leave home in a hurry. I need some help I'm looking for Batavia Street can you help me. He walked to the door said go straight up to the light then, pointing under the interstate, turn left go a few blocks two lights then turn right and you'll find it. Finally, I found Larry's apartment about 7:00 A.M. in the morning just when I was about to give up I'd become discouraged. I thought I'd have to return to that house. Larry came to the door looked me up and down and quietly said love your outfit. I said I think I killed my husband. I tried to get by him but I'm thinking

I hit him with my car. I couldn't get by he blocked me in. I was scared he had a riffle. When he's mad he tries to hurt me and I thought he was going to shoot me. I was not going back with him so in my resistance I'm sure he would have shot me.

I asked to use Larry's phone. I called Jenell's mother to tell her what happened. She said, "he was not dead in the hospital with a hurt hip, some cuts, but he is not dead and has no broken bone." I was relieved. I didn't want him hurt. I didn't want to be married to him any longer, but I did not want him hurt or dead either. Jenell had good qualities, but he was not stable mentally and needed help. Like I said at the time I was not aware, he was on drugs which as I think about it now may account for his sudden brutal behavior then a switch to Mr. nice.

After I calmed down I went out to the car to help Larry get my sleeping child, my dog and the few clothes I was able to gather out of the car.

I don't remember if I asked if I could move in with him or not but suddenly there I was. Only thing his cousin was his roommate but that was quickly remedied. Charles moved next door with their friend. So I was home. Well for a while I was. after about six months Larry began to worried that his father would not be happy with he and I living in the same apartment not married. Yep, there it was again. Nowhere to go, so one more time. Larry was a good guy and I really cared for him so I saw his point he called his mom and she planned our wedding at his home in Ripley. I had a dressmaker I used when I lived in Nashville so I called on her to make me another wedding dress. She said okay, but this is the last one I'll make. She created my last wedding dress worn once by mistake and gotten rid of unfortunately after the wedding instead of before. I should have burned it before the wedding. I was hopeful this dress would be cherished. It was a beautiful blue gown and a beautiful small wedding.

A year later, things were still going good. I had a job at Baptist Hospital and a promise from them to get into the newly formed associate degree nursing program with my tuition paid. I went to the administration when I got to Nashville and asked if how I could get into their graduate nurse program. I was told that program was being phased out. I thought they were just not wanting to let me in, so I said so. There had been, to my knowledge no black nurses ever graduated from that program. At least I saw no blacks in the photos on the wall in class pictures. It turns out the three year programs were really being phased out. Their time had come there was a trend toward having a college degree in nursing this new program was the kick start. The two-year associates degree program was replacing the three-year graduate program. After I finished all the accusations the administrator told me if I would agree to work there three years after graduation they would put me in the next class, pay my tuition and buy my books. I said where do I sign? I was sitting on the Moon with my feet hanging over! Happy, happy, happy. When it was time to enroll somehow I was given an additional scholarship from a doctor in Dickson Tennessee. The terms were: I couldn't get married, miss over two days of class, get pregnant, or make any drastic change during the time I was in school. I worked every weekend to help with expenses so we would survive. Larry was in school, too, so we made it but it was rough. On top of that I was already pregnant when I signed the term agreement. I was determined pregnancy only one infraction out of many would not stop me. I decided not to tell anyone I was pregnant, so as I got bigger and bigger I told people there was a rabbit under my shirt. My classmates would ask how's the rabbit? As I grew bigger and bigger I could not do some of my task. The teachers and the students were nice. They saw how hard I tried and how much I wanted this chance. They really went the distance to help me with clinicals. If a dummy was needed I became the dummy. I was rolled over, helped to stand, positioned, treated as a stroke victim and fed. I could hear the instruction and learn but saved from performing heavy lifting. I was an LPN anyway and this was a refresher for me. I already knew all this stuff but still had to go through clinicals as a new nursing student. If I had to crawl under stuff or reach way up another classmate was immediately on the spot to help. I use to talk to the rabbit to encourage it to come on Friday night or Saturday early so I wouldn't miss school. Third semester just before midterms early. One Saturday morning 2:00 A.M. the rabbit arrived all eight pounds four ounces of her. That evening the doctor came in to see me and I asked to go home. I said the rabbit could stay if she needed, but I had to go get everything ready to return to class on Monday. I told him my head was fine that Bufferin and a pillow would take care of the rest. He paused then said okay, but if you have problems such as bleeding excessively return immediately. I agreed. Just like that I was discharged. The pediatrician came next and he discharged the rabbit. So at 6:00 P.M. that evening we went home. The rabbit was so cute and so healthy. As soon as we got home I called a local radio station. I told them my story and asked for help finding a babysitter quickly. Low and behold they made the request over the air and a young girl replied. She was a little challenged but very able to care for the baby. She came to the house and I watched her with the baby. I told her to just feed the baby and diaper her. I explained that's all you do. She was okay with that and did fine. I did not use pampers. I used cloth diapers, so I taught her to fold the diaper and how to put Vaseline on the baby's bottom to avoid diaper rash. All day Sunday we practiced diapering, feeding, burping and preparing bottles. About 4:00 P.M., I felt she was ready.

Larry left home earlier morning for class and got home before me in the afternoon. This was good cause the sitter was not alone with the baby too long. she was alone about three hours. So the new adventure began. Monday I went back to clinicals making beds and caring for patients at St. Thomas the old St. Thomas Hospital all morning. In the afternoon all students had to go downtown to the college for classes.

When I arrived at the school, the administrator met me in the hall. She asked, "Where's the rabbit?"

I said, "Home eating rabbit food."

She said, "When did the rabbit come out?"

I said, "Saturday morning."

She asked, "What are you doing here?"

I said, "My scholarship hinges on my missing no days or I'll lose it and get put out of school."

She took off up the hall. In a couple of minutes my instructors and the administrator were coming toward me down the hall. One of them drug a desk out and I was told to sit. The next thing I knew I was handed test from all my classes. I forgot it was midterm week. It was incredible the instructors came by my desk and said it's not A, B, or C, so what do you think the answer is? A weeks' worth of midterm exams took about thirty minutes and the instructors virtually helped me decide many of the answers. On top of that the administrator said your class mates and this faculty want the rabbit to have rabbit food, so we collected money for her. We also think you should go home and be with the rabbit. There were 101 students in the class each gave two dollars each and the faculty gave as well, so they gave me almost $300. I was floored. This money was so needed both Larry and I worked, but we were still struggling and juggling bills. Gotta say without a doubt though Larry was one of the hardest working men I have ever met. He helped with the baby, cleaned the house and even cooked when needed and never missed a day school. He slept very little and worked so much I worried about his health.

One evening we were eating when I got a call from Jenell. He said my name was on some papers that had me owning a piece of his property and he needed me to sign it back to him. I did not want anything I did not earn, so I said fine. Larry was not overjoyed but was okay with me going, so we met. The meet was in Jenell's hotel room in Nashville. As I think back this was not a wise idea. Jenell wanted to talk and talk. He did his best to convince me I still loved him and should come back to him. I had to do fancy footwork to avoid him being all over me. Understand when Jenell was being nice he was heart stopping handsome and so, so smooth. I'm a good dancer.

Danced around and dodged the best. I kept my underwear up, my clothes on and Jenell got his papers all signed. Great work for one night. Can't say I did not think about his offers sex and money because I had way less money than he could give me, and my sex meter was severely low. Larry was not interested in sex daily and weekly was iffy. The way Larry worked even sex monthly was a stretch. The saving grace was I had more than money now not much sex, but I had happiness. That was the last time I ever saw Jenell.

Things were going good. Larry and I were happy but so broke one evening we were without lights and we were without food. Our school refund checks were due to be in the next day. His mother called to see how we were that evening we said we're fine. Actually we were not. We had milk for the baby that's all. My older daughter was away at college and there were no other children at that time. Larry and I shared a package of Ramen Noodles. We never let anyone know how broke we were.

Finally, we graduated. Larry graduated first. I had to pay back the contracted portion of my student loan, so I went to work at Baptist Hospital. On Two East there remained a sign over the water fountains in front of my desk. It said white only. I quickly took it down. Seems no one ever missed it. There was only one occasion as I recall that it seemed a person had a problem with me running a floor. This was early seventies and things were slowly changing in the south. A women saw me and a white technician sitting at the desk. I was in white head to toe with a nurse's cap on. My technician just had on white no cap not even a name tag. The women explained her problem that required a nurse about a patient thoroughly to my technician who listened intently then she said you need to speak to the charge nurse and pointed over at me. The lady looked at me for a response to her problem. I replied I'm sorry I was not listening just to make her repeat it because she knew I was a nurse in the first place yet chose to ignore me. This never happened again. As a matter of fact, I had a delightful time working there.

While Larry was waiting to hear from any of his applications to a Medical College he went to work with his dad in Memphis. While he was gone I found a house that was perfect for our family. I made application for a loan. I used Larry's name and his dad's address because that was where Larry was at the time. Somehow the loan company got Larry and his dad's name mixed up and the loan went through in his dad's name. His dad had established great credit. No I didn't even try to straighten it out. At the closing we corrected the spelling of Larry's name that's all. It was fabulous, unbelievable life even got better. Then along comes Jones. A year later Larry decided to allow his sister to come and stay with us until she found a job. That was okay with me she was looking for a job. She was an educator, so I figured how long could the stay be? Can't remember who said it but it's true fish and guess laying around stink after three days. Try six months. If you're a houseguest one or two weeks you may not help do anything around the house in which you are staying, but if your stay becomes your residence after six to eight months you make your bed, wash a dish, sweep a floor do something to earn your keep. She shared a room with my older daughter and acted as if she had a maid. Dalise had to keep the room clean Larry would have died if it was dirty, so my daughter was left cleaning up after our eight-month house guest. I talked with Larry about it. I asked if he would at least have her make up her bed. He said, no she was company. At six months your no longer company you are a boarder, at eight months' rent is due. Didn't want money from her just wanted her to join in on the housekeeping and not even the whole house just the room she shared. Cooking and cleaning other rooms I could handle. This became a real problem. It was clear Larry was more concerned that he not cause her worry but me he didn't mind. Small matter I know but just enough to wear away like dripping water on a salt block leaving cracks in a good marriage. I'm easy. I'm always looking for the good in others. I love fully I trust completely, but when I or if I feel I have to protect myself or those in my care. I change. I'm not hard headed you hurt me, you don't value me, if I'm threatened I can turn love off like a porch light. This porch was becoming dim. Finally, she got a job in another state and was gone. By then, the damage was done. I was hurt by all of this and Larry couldn't see reason. I understand it better now I'm older, lived more, but then I did not. Larry and his sister felt like they were on their own and all they had was each other, so Larry protected her. They were taken from their mother and made to live with grandparents, the father's family. When their dad came home from the Marines he pulled them from there plopped in a house with him a stern father and his new wife, a step mother, who he demanded they call Mom. They were not able to speak about or permitted to see their real mother, who lived about eight blocks away, again. That's a lot to handle for little kids, so the two of them grew up holding on to and protecting each other. Way, way too late, years later, I understood. When it mattered I did not. I just felt I had been treated second class, stepped on and ignored. I saw his behavior as allowing his sister to use me and saw him as mean with a total lack of respect for my feelings. I'm sure Larry was not aware of it but some of the bitterness Larry had was a carryover from his past relationship with his dad. That dark side like an ugly beast roared out at the oddest times. One night I had taken off a sanitary napkin in the bathroom. I wrapped it and put it in a bag and through it in the bathroom trash. Larry had a fit. Insisted even at night a bag with a pad in it be taken outside to the trash. He said when he lived with his real mother he saw her walk through the house with blood on the back of her nightgown going into her bedroom with some strange guy. It made little sense to me. It was so long ago that it should have been forgotten. It was important to him definitely not forgotten. It sure messed him up. After a while, I discovered there were many ghost in Larry's past that still haunted him. He didn't care that he yelled and screamed at people if their view differed from his. Larry lived in a very narrow mental box his way of thinking period. It was as if two people lived in his body one quiet, sweet and shy, the other with a total lack of compassion. He and I were driving one Saturday when an old man and his dog were walking across the street the dog must have been old cause he was walking slow. From all I could see Larry did not slow down to allow them to pass. He made no effort not to hit the dog. I saw the dog jump or was flung toward the curb. Larry did not stop. Never slowed. Whether he did or did not hit the dog I don't know. It was the comment that sickened me. I said that could have been that old man's only friend they are old. Why didn't you slow down and give them a chance to pass? He said, "He gotta get out the street." That incident was the middle of the end. It took away the last love I had for him. I don't get joy from others pain and I have a problem with anyone who is careless about causing it unnecessarily. It was clear Larry had escalating mental issues. I could see it. We all have our demons but his were becoming life size. I was in the bedroom one evening when I heard a loud deep voice yelling at my oldest daughter. I came to the kitchen to see what was happening. It was Larry yelling. I had never heard him raise his voice. I waited until Dalise left the room and I asked what was that about. He responded so nasty that I went to the bed room and stood looking at the baby sleep. I don't remember what the argument grew to, but I remember him hitting me and me falling over the bassinet knocking it over and the baby rolling to the floor. I picked the baby up, checked to see if she was hurt and held her tight to try to stop her from crying. Larry left the room. This was so out of character for him. I learned later he had been turned down for Meharry Medical School that week. Maybe he was angry for being rejected and just taking it out on those in reach. I urged him to apply to other colleges and he said he would, but I'm not certain he ever did.

Probably not related to the fall but soon after that incident Pete, the rabbit, began to have seizures. At first it was the kind of seizure that her eyes rolled up and her chest lifted from the bed. I began sleeping on the floor next to her crib so I could be there at the first sign of a seizure. Larry was working nights at a bakery and many is the night he would arrive home right after or during the baby having had a seizure. I would be standing in the drive with the baby in my arms and I'd hop in the car when he stopped. We would rush her to the emergency room at least two to three times a month. We had a wonderful pediatrician he would meet us any time of the night. This went on for years.

The Rabbit was about six years old, it was Christmas Eve and she was in an angel costume for a role in a Christmas play. As soon as I got the wings and halo on right she had to use the bathroom. Tired as I was I said go. After just a few minutes in the bathroom I heard the metal from the wings hitting the porcelain sink or toilet couldn't tell which. It was in a repeated tapping sound. I ran to the bathroom and there she was head caught between the sink and toilet. I was panicked I screamed for Larry. He ran in the bathroom took one look, did not hesitate just bent over and pulled the toilet out of the floor. Until this day I do not know where he got the strength. He pulled the toilet from the bolts in the floor water went everywhere and I pulled her free. If he had not gotten her head out she would have snapped her neck. She had fallen from the toilet having a grand mal seizure and her head was caught between the sink console and commode. The force of the convulsions was causing the wings to tap on my towel rack that had fallen over on her. That was the noise I heard. The guy who acted so quickly and direct that's the Larry I knew and loved. The other one was strange and mean. I decided this was a dangerous way to live and definitely not a way to raise children, so I tried moving out of the house. He found my apartment and created such distraction it caused the manager to put me out. Couldn't get food stamps. He told DHS I left him and he was perfectly able to support his family. So I moved back in and slept in another room most of the time. Between mad and make up we had two more children. I believe after we were married those were the three times we had sex. Yeah, three, maybe four usually again on Christmas Eve. Seems he was happy during the holidays. He loved to decorate and we both loved looking at all the toys which usually stretched into the center of the entire floor. Unfortunately, Larry was not much on sex which was part of our problem. He would rather sleep in the bathtub than in bed. No he was not impotent just didn't seem to care at all about cuddling, or sex. Couple the lack of intimacy with fighting often about very little. The marriage was spiraling into a disaster. We argued about almost everything except the kids. Larry became so jealous living with him was like jail

One night I went shopping with a girlfriend after we stopped shopping we went to eat, so I got home late about 10:45 P.M. Larry locked the house doors. I had no key for the new locks. I had to sleep in my car. He opened the door as he left for work. After that if the kids and I we were out our older daughter would be frightened to return home if we stayed out after dark. She grabbed at my clothes and I could feel her body shaking as we came through the door. The first time that happened I knew I had to get us out of there, but I had no money and no safe place to go. I used to give my paycheck unopened to Larry and wrote checks for our needs. I did not suffer for anything just didn't have control of my money. That was okay, too, because I was pretty bad at not spending and bills may have been left off if I was the one paying them. One thing I can say in his behalf, Larry was a great provider and an excellent father. He just did not understand how to treat a women or wife. He thought head of the house meant keep your wife obedient, no opinion and pregnant. Didn't mind the pregnant part the no opinion was a problem. I believe he was getting bad advice from friends or his father. The concept of barefoot and pregnant may have worked when women were better off seeking a profitable Mrs. instead a possible BS by going to college, working and finding their own way. Not that I didn't want a great provider in a man, I did, but I wanted to be valued for my accomplishments and my opinion considered, too.

I made up my mind I had to leave. Now I needed money above my paycheck to do it.

I met a nice guy at work easy to talk with and fun to be around. I began to go over his house in the mornings after I cleaned the house and put dinner on. It was great to have a guy and friend to talk with and on occasion borrow a cup of sex from. No love it just felt good to have someone hold me and say nice things. Having a women friend was okay I thought men understood things better and in this case fill a dual purpose.

I would always ask Larry to go to the staff parties or to a dance, but at the last minute I'd be dressed to go and he would make fun of my dress or say ugly things anything to back out of going. He wasn't very social, so instead Tom and I would attend staff parties. That man looked great in clothes and could dance. Tom was fun, very social and a great friend, but had no potential. He was broke most of the time and didn't want to go to college. He could not help me financially, so he and I just enjoyed each other's company. Tom had no girlfriend by choice I'm sure. cause he was nice looking and very popular. As time went on Larry and I did not talk much and did not have sex but a few times a month, if that so Tom became a frequent go to for that as well. So much so that when I found out I was pregnant again I wondered who's was it. Since Larry and I had not had sex on an ongoing basis I thought there is a possibility it may not be his. I figured I could not pass that off as his if it wasn't and besides I did not want any more children anyway. I was trying to leave. I heard about this place that offered help to women who wanted abortions. Since it was illegal in this town they arranged it out of town. The office was above the Gas company down town second floor there was an office that arranged for those who wanted abortions to travel to New York on a one-day trip have it done and return home by that evening. I made the arrangements and Tom gave me the money. I had to travel in the evening so someone would be home with my child. I was a student, so I used my student pass to cut the cost of the flight to New York. I arrived after the clinic closed, so I had to stay over until the morning when they opened and I could catch the shuttle. I slept in LaGuardia

Airport on a bench. Some pilots came through late in the evening about midnight and noticed me asleep on the bench. They told me no flights were leaving this late tonight. I said I know I'm just sleeping here tonight no money for a hotel. They asked had I eaten. I said come with us. We walked to the staff lounge where there was plenty of food. I ate well and since I had no money for a hotel, so I returned to the bench to sleep. The guys gave me blanket and I slept well.

The next morning, I boarded the shuttle. It delivered me to the clinic where I was shuffled from area to area, questioned to see if I was of sound mind and wanted to truly do this. When I finished that line of procedures I was handed a gown told to remove my clothes from the waist down. I undressed and was put on a table in knees up legs open position. There was a room full of tables with women on them like the one I was on all in a row. The doctor and nurse just moved from table to table until they reached me. A speculum was inserted in my vagina then a catheter with strong suction. I felt a big cramp in my stomach and then like my whole insides were being sucked out into that machine before it stopped. Then they moved on. They pulled me flat slapped a giant pad from my back to my navel between my legs and I was rolled to a room given juice and told to rest. Twenty minutes later a voice came over a speaker and announced the next shuttle would be here in ten minutes those on the 1:00 P.M. flight needed to dress to go. I was given another large pad told to change and directed to the waiting area. I got on the shuttle and made my flight. I heard the sounds and remember seeing some of the larger building from the bus coming and going to the clinic that's all. That was my experience and second visit to the Big Apple. I got home about 3:00 P.M. cooked dinner, picked the baby up from the sitter, did homework and went to bed. Larry acted like he never knew I was gone. We were arguing when I left so he didn't miss me. Nothing changed overnight. As with most nights Larry slept on the sofa or in the bath tub. The next night he came in while I was asleep woke me up kissing my legs and stomach. We made sex. Don't think it was love on his part it certainly wasn't on my part just need. This nightly storm of sex went on for about a week and bang I was pregnant again. I think that's what he wanted. Larry liked it when I was pregnant.

I had just joined the Air Guard, but when I got called I was pregnant at that time they made those pregnant come back after the baby was born. A year went by my baby was three months old when I tried this time. The recruiter looked up at me and said your too old, too short, and too fat. I weighed 179 pounds, was thirty-five years old, and I was four and a half feet tall. She said we will hold this paperwork one month. I said I have one month to lose forty pounds? She said yes your weight must be 139 or less. one month till my paperwork expired, so I had to lose forty pounds, get younger and stretch two feet. No problem. I was so determined I turned to a zero carb diet. I ate lettuce, ground beef and green peppers three meals a day and cheese only as a snack. I did not even use sugar free gum or toothpaste. I brushed with baking soda and Listerine. I ran every morning six times around Bordeaux hospital. In twenty-nine days, I returned to the recruiter to swear in. The recruiter did not recognize me. I said, I'm too short, too old, and I'm too fat remember. She said, what did you do to get so thin? I said sign me up. I went from 179 pounds to 109 pounds. I lost seventy pounds in one month. I got a waiver for my height and my education waived my age to twenty-five. I had to be dropped from rank of captain to first Lieutenant. My age would have demanded Captain if I was thirty-five years old, but now I was twenty-five years old that's first Lieutenant Rank. The change put me in line to serve twenty years otherwise I would have to get out cause of age before I made twenty. I was scheduled to leave for basic the next month. Three days before I shipped out I was at a local car wash with my three-month-old baby and my seventeen-month-old daughters. my hair had just been washed and it stood all over my head. I was in old raggedy shorts and flip flops trying to get change from the machine to wash my car. The machine would not give me change. This guy in a yellow corvette pulled up. I thought he was the owner. I asked him for change. He asked, the machine is out? I said it's not working. He said follow me I'll wash your car. I thought we were heading for another car wash. I followed him and we ended up at his house. We got out he got the hose and I stood back with the kids watching him spray the car. All of a sudden he sprayed me and the kids. Oh, I'm sorry he said. Come in put your stuff in the dryer. I redressed the baby from the diaper bag, put the older girls' things in the dyer and put a small t shirt on her that he gave me. I, too, put on one of his bigger Tee shirt which made a dress on me. He was a big guy, so his shirts were very big on me. I fed the kids while he finished the car. He took so long the kids fell asleep on the sofa while he was waxing the car. He finished the car came in showered and sat on his bed to dress. He invited me into his room since the kids were spiraled over the sofa, to watched T.V. from his very unique red round bed. One minute we were having a conversation like old married people the next we were making love like newlyweds in his big round bed. He had to weigh two hundred pounds or more, but he was so sweet, gentle and careful not to smash me. A handsome man with strong arms, beautiful teeth, a big laugh and an infectious smile. We just clicked. I told him my situation and he listened for a long time then he said why are you there? I told him what had happened. I loved my husband, but it was getting hard to live with him. There was no sex, no love, increased fighting over small stuff and not much conversation between us. On top of that I feared he had an undiagnosed mental problem for which he refuses to seek any concealing or evaluation. I shared with him about the night I woke up with Larry pointing a .30-06 six rifle at my head. Then how he ran out of the house to the street as I opened my eyes and shot out all the street lights. I told him sleeping with a complete stranger was not a usual occurrence, but Larry I had not made love since I became pregnant with that baby and that was now twelve months ago and before that only rarely. That pregnancy was on a week's binge of sex on a makeup after a mad. I enjoy sex and I missed having the closeness, so I told him I had a friend who pinch hits but not like this. This was fabulous out of my mind kind of wonderful. I really liked this guy. He seemed fun we laughed and talked all afternoon. He fixed me lunch and said can you have dinner or drinks with me later.

I said, "I'll try. Frankly I never expected you to want to see me again. I thought this was a one afternoon thing, a fun while it lasted."

He said, "Oh, no."

I said, "I have to go; it's getting late."

As I was leaving, I said, "What's your name?"

He replied, "MacElron, like macaroni."

That night I fixed my hair and put on a sun dress and went to the restaurant where he said to meet him down town. He walked past me twice before he recognized me.

He said, "Wow, you are beautiful. I didn't recognize you." We had dinner and we talked. I told him I joined the Air Force and I was leaving for basic training in two days. He asked why I wanted to do that. I told him I needed an income to support myself above my pay from nursing. I planned to divorce my husband and live alone me and the kids. He paused then ordered more cokes; he did not drink, nor did I.

He said, "Are you going to forget me?"

I said, "No, are you going to find someone else at the car wash while I'm gone?"

He leaned over and kissed me and said, "There is no one else for me. I like washing your car, and the benefits are good."

I got his address and promised to write. He said, "I'll come to Texas, if it's okay."

I kissed him goodbye and went home. No he did not own the car wash. Don't know what he was doing there. He was a smooth talking Trailways bus driver. It felt good being with someone who made mad crazy love again, had money, was single free and easy and made spontaneous decisions like me.

Two days later I took the kids to their grandma in Memphis and flew to Texas for the first leg of my basic training. Freedom.

My first encounter with Shepard Air Force Base began on the plane going there. I met this nice man we talked the entire way there. I told him I had no uniforms, so I didn't know how I was going to get one before I had to report in. He said you will get uniforms don't worry about money and buying them. You'll be fine. When we arrived he asked where I was going. I said I don't really know I guess to sign in. He said my wife is picking me up would you like a ride? I said sure I have no idea how I am to get to or if I even have the right Place. His wife and kids came and off we went. When I got to housing I noticed everyone the stood up as we walked in. I thought what gentleman standing for a lady that was nice. I got the paperwork and the man said let me see it. I gave him the papers he seemed to know more about this than me. He, I and his wife were wondering over the barracks trying to find my assigned quarters. When we finally found them they did not appear well kept. He went in first, carrying my bags and came out quick and said these are not good. Let's go get a better one. Being new didn't want to complain sounding wimpy, so I said they may get mad at me. He said it's okay this is not good you don't want to stay here. Back we went to Billeting and this time he went in and his wife and I sat in the car and talked. Sure enough he came out with a new for new quarters. The new apartment was a block away a nice building on the front upstairs of the building and nice. I thanked them for the help and for being so patient. I tried to pay him a small fee.

He said, "I'll see you at the club; buy me a drink."

I said, "Deal."

My second encounter was when I reported in by then I weighed one hundred pounds and the nurse at Shepard said I was too thin and asked me to be sure I ate or I would be sent to the infirmary for an examination to see if I was malnourished. If I mistreated government property by starving that was an offense. I was so used to not eating it was a chore to eat and I ran track three miles out of habit two times a day.

I returned to my quarters and began to organize my stuff and in walked another girl.

She asked, "Are you sure you have the right apartment?"

I said, "Yeah, I think so."

She asked, "Is this a two-person apartment?" This was 1976, and she was white and had a strong Mississippi accent.

I said, "Yes, I guess we're housemates."

She said, "I've never had a roommate before; which room is mine?"

I said, "Either; I took the first one, but I can move.

She said, "No, it's okay."

We got talking and she said, "I never have been this close to a colored person before that wasn't a servant."

I said, "Why not?"

She said, "I don't know. We had colored people who worked for our family, but they lived somewhere else. I never shared housing or even school with a colored person before."

This is different. She was just staring at me.

I said, "Feel me, I'm real. It's okay, we are going to have fun."

I sensed she was kind of afraid of me. I found out later she was wondering what her father would think her living with a colored housemate. After the ice broke we talked for hours. I learned she was very rich, drove a Porsche and joined the Air Force because shortly after marrying a prominent bank president. Seems she went home, out of state, to visit with her family and to get some of her belongings she wanted to move to her newly built home. She returned to her new home early. Her husband should have been at work but he was home and to her surprise and his I'm sure to find her husband and his boyfriend busy in her new bed. Her husband was a Bank President who only needed a wife for appearances and to attend special events. He had a boyfriend for sexual happiness. In 1976 gay was not acceptable especially for a bank president, so he married a woman for appearances. He hid but kept the boyfriend. She said she and her husband made a deal. Her husband would pay her a tidy sum to remain absent, but stay married. It was easier for him to explain her absence if she were in the military. So there we were the odd couple. We un-packed and she decided we should drive around and see what Wichita had to offer. We quickly discovered if there was to be fun we had to make it. That was the beginning. I made lots of friends and drug her reluctantly right along with me. At first she was like a deer in head-lights, but soon she was partying like the rest of us. One night in the jammed packed club from across the dance floor possible after way too many drinks she yelled if my daddy could see me now! We had a group who were all party animals. I didn't drink don't think anyone realized it because I danced more, acted crazier and was louder than anyone else in the group. I was labeled ring leader. When we began meeting at the club it was dead, but not for long. The new kids were in town and everywhere we went the party was on. The O Club at-tendance was improving every night but on Wednesday night it was off the chain. People just began showing up. I don't believe all of us were officers but all were in civilian clothes, so who knew. The place got jammed packed. We danced until they closed it down, put out the lights, unplugged the juke box literally making us leave. So much for the dead base others had described. We partied hard and we worked hard. We got up at O-dark thirty each morning ran three miles had chow, went to class and it started all over that evening. I loved it. I was free, had money and good friends. Not that I didn't get in trouble I did. Once on a walk I discovered a plane covered with a tight tarp, and the area roped off with yellow banners. I failed to understand the yellow ribbon meant restricted area everyone keeps away. I thought they meant no non-military people could be there. I was curious, so I pulled the tarp back and wow there was this plane shaped like a triangle it was beautiful comparing it today it looked like a stealth. I whipped out my camera and took a picture. In seconds or sooner I was face down on the pavement with a gun to my head and a boot on my back. Someone took my camera and someone snatched me to my feet. I was sharply asked what was I doing? I ex-plained I took a walk and there was this thing I uncovered it and it was a plane. I took a picture of it. I thought it was beautiful. I told him I had not ever seen a plane like that. I was advised that I was in a restricted area for which I had no clearance and it should not happen again and was rushed on my way without my camera. Scary time. I did not venture to that end of the base again. I did buy a new camera which again proved to be a mistake for a whole other reason, but I'll talk more about that later.

The next day, I was in class learning who to salute and who to pea on in walks this entourage the instructor shouted Aten hut! We stood to attention. In walks my bag caring friend from the plane only this time he was in a uniform and lots of metals on his chest. The instructor introduced him as General someone, the Base Commander.

He said, "At ease."

In the next breath, he said, "I want all of your new officers to be comfortable, and if you have problems, call on me. I already know one of you." She had me bag dragging all over the base to find her suitable quarters. Looking at me he said, "I trust you are comfortable, Lieutenant?"

I said, "Very much, sir."

He said, "You still owe me that drink."

I replied, "Yes, sir."

I had no idea this man was anything on the plane he had on shorts and deck shoes. I was so outdone. If I could have turned red I would have. I have to admit it was fun to think I had the Base Commander caring my bags and his wife who was sweet chauffeuring little ole me around base. It was a fabulous way to be introduced to military life. The memory of that day is still warm when I think of him taking the time to help me a stranger not feel lost, show concern about getting me better quarters I tear up with pride. This was a two-star general, and he was actually a nice guy. I think that was the day I fell in love with the military. It was a family. That was a fun time lots of new rules but fun. I was coming out of the post office on a one-hundred-degree afternoon when I saw another soldier in a uniform. I thought he might have been army but I did not recognize the rank. Well I said hello and he said Lieutenant how do military greet one another? I immediately saluted. In the front of a busy post office I held that salute for all of five minutes in a 100-plus degree weather. I could see other troops laughing at me as I stood at attention holding a salute. Finally, he dropped his salute and walked away. Everyone cheered. I was so embarrassed. I Still did not know his rank. I'm told he was a ranger and a Bird Col. and as a first lieutenant I should have saluted him first because his rank outranked mine. I just wanted to disappear, so I took a short cut through the gulf course through the grass hoping no one would see me. This was the shortest distance to my quarters. Half way through the field taps sounded, so I had to stop face the music and salute. I did, and yep, you guessed it; the sprinkler system came on. I was in the middle of a field by then, in uniform wet and could not move. I looked like a drowned rat by the time I got to my quarters. This was not a good day, but it was lessons learned. My instructor saw me on the way into my apartment and said welcome to the military. Those were two lessons but I learned many more valuable lessons before I left Shepard.

As all good things do this leg of my tour ended. It was time for graduation and on to survival and flight training. Some of us were shipped through together all of us were not. I was shipped to Brooks AFB in San Antonio, Texas, alone. These quarters were paired side by side with a shared kitchen. I had a new housemate. She was standing in her room door open playing the song Easy like Sunday morning a song I had never heard, so I moseyed over there to listen. There stood Anna a normally attractive woman with her eyes closed swaying to the song. She turned when I entered to introduced herself.

Then she said, "I'm Anna. I have a problem; I have nymphomania. Do you know what that is?" Before I could get over the shock and answer she said, "If you have a man, you really like do not introduce him to me. I will sleep with anybody it won't matter if he's your guy or the garbage man. I get headaches if I go without sex very long."

I said, "How long is long?"

She said, "Like you must have food, I have to have sex."

I said, "Oh."

She said, "For real, close the doors between the kitchen and our rooms if you have company. I don't want to hear or see him, okay?"

I said, "Works for me."

We understood each other and became friends who could talk to one another about most things. Seems like a lot of the women I met in the military so far were escaping something or somebody. All had a reason to be where they were with no wish to go back. I learned early in life if it says it bites it bites, so I took Anna at her word. Some of our running buddies didn't believe fat meat was greasy and made the mistake of thinking she was kidding and would introduce Anna to their boyfriends. Mistake! It did not take long before their so-called wonderful boyfriend was coming out of Anna's apartment either early morning or late night looking very tired but with a smile. Then the girlfriend wanted to get mad at Anna. I'd say not Anna's fault she warned you and you still introduced then told your boyfriend about her. Besides, that guy knew and had free will. He didn't have to go to her apartment he chose to. Anna lost a few friends like that, but that didn't stop her. She must have been careful in her go rounds because she had no children and no diseases. Anna was the only person I ever met who admittedly was a nymphomaniac. I've met some women who were close but were just sleep arounders with no psychological disease. The difference was they were not as aggressive as Anna. She didn't have to like the guy, didn't want money or even to know his name. She didn't even want conversation. She was the original wham, bam, thank you, ma'am. Five minutes after they were finished she wanted him gone and probably wouldn't recognize the guy she just churned all over the bed, floor or kitchen table with if she saw his face on the street. His looks were not what held her interest. She had sexual desire like a vampire craves blood. When she met a guy she only paid attention to his cleanliness and his zipper size. She used the guy like a black widow spider except she didn't kill him. She just used him till he couldn't function anymore. When he couldn't get it up he was put out. Anna has no emotion about her victims at all. Bet she could do six or seven guys a day more if she had access and time.

I often wonder what became of her. I shipped out home she opted for an overseas tour. We never met again. I liked her because she was honest with no pretenses. I had not nor have I since met anyone so basic or so purely honest. Anna, as all humans do, had animal instincts which most of us try to suppress, she didn't bother. Anna acted on her instincts and because of her behavior, she was viewed as a misfit. The more I think about it the more I wonder was she or is society misfit? All I know is after knowing her I go with my instincts even more.

This was a special time. This was survival school. I learned many things here. I already felt my entire life had been a training camp for survival but still I learned much more. Sleeping in a tent with men and women in war simulated conditions I learned to value quiet and not to rattle my dog tags cause my fellow soldiers got irritated when waken by careless noise. I learned early to avoid irritating anyone, so one night trying not to wake anyone I clutched my tags and slipped out of the tent to use the latrine which was a hole in the ground down wind of the tents. I made it got over the hole squatted down but as I rose with toilet tissue still in hand pants below my knees I was staring at very two very shinny boots. In them was Sgt. Martinez.

"Good evening, ma'am," he said, "where is your partner?"

Wiping quickly, I explained, "I did not want to wake anyone. They were tired, so I came alone."

He said, "That was real neighborly of you. I will escort you through this war torn danger zone to your tent."

Once there he began to bang on all the tent poles waking everyone immediately. In a kind voice he explained this fine officer was in a danger zone alone, with no lookout. She did not want to disturb any of you by asking for help and waking anyone up.

He said, "The latrines seem to be too far away. We need to fix that, so please arise so we can fix that problem. Let's see, I know you all can help by digging six more latrines by 6:00 A.M., closer to the tent so no one will have to walk so far or bother their partner to go with them next time."

I knew we were never to be without a buddy for lookout in a war zone on a mission, so at 2:00 A.M. in the morning we were all issued shovels. What a night. I could feel the anger, but no one said a word we just dug in silence. Needless to say that I never went anywhere without a partner again. We moved camp site at first light the next day, so we never got to use our newly dug latrines. Oddly enough no one acted too mad at me. They weren't happy, but they understood we were all new and learning.

We were brand new Air Force being trained by seasoned Marines. We were learning the personal difficulties that went with going through enemy lines to stabilize and transport wounded Marines. After two weeks in what was very close to a desert setting no water unless your canteen was full or it was dipped from a standing puddle, no food unless you killed it and no MREs. We were told we could eat armadillo if we caught one; unfortunately, we never caught one. After two days without food we were given about a pound of dirty meat Sgt. Martinez, said he accidentally, dropped in the mud. We were so hungry we didn't care. We quickly cleaned it up put it in a pot, added potatoes wild onion and salt tablets boiled it over open an open fire and made soup. Not bad I discovered when you are hungry a little dirt only acts as a filler. My skin was covered in bites my hair was matted and I had not undressed and bathed in two weeks. We were taught the smell of soap or smelly lotion could alert the enemy to your position. I had slithered through mud over and under wire with what I believed was live ammo being fired at me. We camped one night near a small body of water. While we were near water and a fire I took the opportunity to wash my face and feet without soap. I hadn't removed my boots in two days. My feet were sore and my heels were raw from sleeping in my boots. I'm sure I smelled awful, but who could tell we all looked and probably smelled the same. When we hot mited (directed) helicopters they slung mud, dust, rocks and water if it was raining dust if it was dry. We walked over sand and crawled over rocky hills sometimes with, we were told, live rounds spitting overhead. We slivered helmet down and butt wiggling through holes, slept standing up when or if opportunity allowed. That was Survival two long weeks of pure torture, but I made it. I had two ticks on me and mosquito bites everywhere, but if I reported it I would have had to be treated back at base and then return to do this tour all over again. I threatened anyone who thought about reporting me. I'll just die here I said not going back to base. No way I wanted to go through that training again.

When it was finally over we pilled on a bus and headed out. The bus dumped us and our gear on our street. I dragged myself to my door and stripped naked down to the dirty socks before I went in. I showered at least an hour. I think I had enough dirt on me to plant something. At least that part of survival training was ended. I returned to base a changed individual. I had even more determination and I was definitely stronger. I was awarded the Bitch and Moan award at debriefing because I complained about my hair daily and wanting my curlers which kept everyone laughing. This was an eye opening experience. I was certain about one thing if I had to go into a war zone I wanted to have Sgt. Martinez on board. He was pure Marine. He said to me once when I thought I could not walk another step especially not up a hill in rain and mud with twenty pounds of gear on my back, "Ma'am, it's mind over matter. I don't mind and you don't matter. The mission is all. Let's move. Let's get up that hill."

Dragging and miserable as I was I found the strength and up the hill I climbed. He was on the ground in the mud with me staring in my face. Sgt. Martinez saw all of us like a mother hen. He saw everything and seemed to be everywhere. He was a credit to himself and the corps I'd go to war with him anytime. He was awesome. I know he would not babysit but he would keep the troops motivated enough to stay alive. I don't recall ever seeing him smile. I hope he was using his game face during our training, but really was a happy guy. Don't know.

I was in love with the military before survival but after that experience I grew respect. This was not an easy job it took inner strength just to cope.

Our time at Brooks was not all work we had some down time after our return. My crew and I went to a party to celebrate making it through survival. It was off base at one of the guy's apartment. It was fun. I did not drink but that night I had a glass of wine. It made me so sleepy I crawled to a corner in the room and fell asleep on the carpet. About 3:00 A.M. in the morning, I woke up and there was not a sound and no one there. I went to the bedroom to see if the host was there he was and sound asleep.

I shook him and said, "You have to get me back to base."

He said, "What are you still doing here?"

I said, "I fell asleep in the corner and no one woke me up; they just left."

He couldn't believe I was still there and slept through all that noise. He said he passed out early mostly from being tired. Reluctantly he got up and was nice enough to drive me back to base. Another lesson learned at parties CYA don't fall asleep cause you're on your own. Everyone minds theirs. The group I was with thought I left with someone. I've always been independent but the military was teaching me a new kind of independence called CYA (cover your ass). Look out for yourself, expect the unexpected, and stay alert at all times.

My time grew short basic training was over and it was time for me to make a decision to return home or not. Although I missed my kids I had no excitement about losing my freedom in a lonely marriage and leaving this freer life. I wanted to opt for a tour overseas, but I knew I could not cause of the kids, so I said my goodbyes and caught a flight home. I called Randall to pick me up from the airport. I was happy to see him again. he had promised to come visit me but instead we wrote a lot. Once he failed to write me in two days, so I wrote him a nasty letter on toilet tissue. He said he laughed so hard because no one had ever mailed him such a letter. He kept it. He said it was one of his prize possessions. He was as handsome and jolly as I remembered. He wanted to change shirts and take me to lunch. He said he was not permitted to wear the uniform anywhere other than while working.

We drove to his hotel and he showered. When he walked out from the bedroom shirt in hand I snapped a picture. This was when a hairy chest was sexy, and he had a big beautiful chest with silky black hair. Today that's not sexy, but then it made for a smoking hot body. I loved petting the straight black hair on his chest. He put the shirt on and we went to eat. We returned to the hotel and spent the day and that night in bed. We talked, we watched T.V.V we ate, we made love. It was a great home coming. Never dawn on me to ask why he was in a hotel room in the same town with his house. As I think about the first time I was at his house there were ladies' garments and curling irons in the bathroom. When I questioned him about them he said his brother and his girlfriend lived there too, so I guess I thought he wanted us to be alone. I don't remember what I thought, if anything. I was wrapped tied, and blinded by him. I thought I could have stayed in that room with him away from the rest of the world for ever. New emotion is like a comfort food it's temporary, aids in loss of reason and makes you feel warm and fuzzy. Fortunately, Randall had to work the next morning because I needed to leave and arrive home. Can't remember how I made that happen, but I did. I believe I caught a cab. My first stop was not home though. I stopped at a lawyer's office down town to file for divorce first. Then I went home. I was not able to deal with Larry one more day. Great father and all that but he and I just were not working. Larry was a fabulous provider which made it hard to call it quits, all things considered I was just miserable so I would seek comfort in someone else. This was not fair to Larry. He deserved someone who was in love with him and I'd rather have all my eggs in one basket. I figured it was better for the kids to have two happy parents living apart rather than hear and see their parents argue and fight together. I always thought I would have been better off with two parents which gave me pause about leaving Larry and taking the kids, but. I hoped Larry would be friends and he stay close to the kids because he loved them and they adored him.

That was the beginning of several years of war. Larry would take the kids to his parents in Memphis and leave them. I would have to go to Memphis to pick them up. I woke up one night with Larry holding a .30-06 pointed at my head then he ran outside and shot the street lights out. I tried to move but he would come and destroy the apartment such that the manager put me out. I tried to get food stamps cause my income was not ample. He told the food stamp people he was able to support me I just decided to leave home. So of course I was denied. I had dinner with Randall at a hotel Restaurant after dinner I returned to my car. I got in and usually I drive fast but today I just cruses. Half way home three of my tires rolled off and down the interstate. I was fine but my car slid, bumped and fell. The wheels, and underside were messed up. It had to be towed. Now no car, I moved back in the house and slept in a separate room.

My case was not getting heard. My lawyer became a judge, so that case was delayed. The next lawyer died. So that case was delayed another year. During this time Larry began following me and Randall alone or together. I knew this was a problem that would not end well cause both of them had bad tempers and guns.

In the meantime my cousin in Pittsburgh called me to say my mom was on the streetcar with one shoe on. seemingly very confused. I knew then Mom living alone was not a good idea. Eddie was sick not able to help much, Mary lived out of town. So did Leo. There was no one to help her as much as she needed on an ongoing basis. Her house was on a hill. Just going to the store was a problem. She had to get up and down the hill to get the streetcar. I decided it was time for her to be near me. Knowing Mom would never want to live with me I was able to rent her an efficiency apartment in a nice elderly community close by me. Larry rented a truck and we went to

Pittsburgh to pack her up and move her here. Of course she didn't want to leave Pittsburgh and fussed from Pittsburgh to Tennessee twelve hours nonstop. She was so unhappy, but after a few weeks she fell in love with the beauty of her surroundings and a cut guy two doors down named John. She smiled when talking about John and she talked about little else. How he cooked and washed her clothes he said this, he said that. I came over to go to the store and tidy up but often felt I was in the way. I offered her and John to come to dinner when the rest of the family came to visit but John refused. Mom reluctantly came, but was unhappy she wanted John. Her memory had gotten so bad she didn't remember most of the other family members. Everyone wanted Mom to remember them, so everyone kept trying to get her attention. She wasn't eating and I could see that this chatter was confusing her even more. I could feel her anxiety, so halfway through the meal I took her home where John was waiting. She was smiling again. This was good. I believe family is where your heart is comfortable her family was in John now. People keep you from being lonesome they do nothing for loneliness. After thirty years of missing my dad she was again happy, she had John. Her memory of yesterday was fleeting and we were the past. John was the present, new and familiar. He made her smile. Eddie, my brother, was not happy because John cooked bacon and sausage for Mom which was not good for her blood pressure, but that's what he knew to cook and he and Mom were happy eating regular food. I told Eddie. Mom would die of something let it be of happiness. How long does she have left? Let her be. Mom gave and gave let her be. She's been unhappy and alone long enough. Eddie quieted he loved Mom. He just worried the salt in beacon and sausage John was fixing for breakfast would kill Mom. After we talked Eddie saw my point. Remembering the years of missing his wife helped his understanding. Everyone needs happiness.

One afternoon I came to see if Mom needed anything and to clean her apartment. This was a very warm afternoon I knocked and I knocked and waited and waited. Finally, she came to the door dress on backward the tag on her chin moving as she spoke. I said do you need anything from the store. She said no John and I were taking a nap. Embarrassed, I said okay call me if you need me. I skipped asking about cleaning. I could tell I was not wanted. I didn't want to be in the way, so I didn't go over the next day. I wanted her to enjoy being with John. The next morning, I went over John had been trying to get in touch with me all night and couldn't find the number. Mom must have thought she was having indigestion because milk of magnesia was around her mouth. Instead she had suffered a stroke. I panicked called Larry who came right away he picked Mom up and we rushed her to the hospital. Not thinking maybe, I should have waited for the ambulance. I was so scared we took her in our car. She was alert the whole way but could not speak. When we reached the hospital she had gone unconscious. She remained that way for a long time in the hospital. When the doctor told me that he had done all he could and wanted to put her in a nursing home I said no. I will take her to my house. I was pregnant at the time about to deliver in days so temporarily and only until I delivered Mom had to be placed in what I thought was a good skilled facility. As soon as I could I was going to take her out of there and home with me. I sold her belongings and hired sitters to stay around the clock while I couldn't. When I showed up at 2:00 A.M. if they were asleep I fired them. That home got real use to me being there at all hours. The staff must have thought I was a teenager. They paid me no mine as I took notes on their care. It was sad to see caregivers not feeding the helpless and eating their food such as apples as they walked by the trays. Really disgusting was families bringing in lawyers to get the sick person to sign over their parent's property to a person that never even visited them. One lady particular only had an amputation and could have gone home with them. I wish my mom could be awake I'd have packed her out of there so fast. Instead of turning the patients every two hours as needed they diapered and turned them at the end of each shift. They took urine samples for glucose reading from the same urine sitting in the bag eight to sixteen hours sometimes and administered insulin according to that reading. I wonder how many died from insulin overdose. They only turned the individuals at shift change. No wonder the decubitus ulcers smell hit you when you got off the elevator and diabetics did not do well. Mom had a tiny red place on her hip which I was caring for and left orders for my sitters to continue the care. I went into the hospital to deliver my baby and stayed two days. When I left the hospital I sent the baby home and I went to see my mother. That small red place on her hip was a giant hole. I was devastated, so I said a prayer and ask Got to take her home if she were not to get better. She was active and spry and wouldn't want to live like this. At 12:01 A.M. that next morning her spirit left that awful place and made the journey to her eternal home. Now I had to tell John. He had been a prisoner of war long ago and had just received his back pay while Mom was in the hospital. He bought Mom an engagement ring and put it on her hand. When I saw the ring on Mom's hand and John just sitting at her bedside staring at her I became sad. I thought about all the time lost. All the unhappy years Mom had and now when she could be happy, this. I tried to comfort John. I told him how sweet this was and asked him to remove the ring. I explained he should propose when Mom woke up. Inwardly I feared the ring would get stolen while she was like this. More importantly Mom would love to receive the ring and hear John say I love you. Now I had to tell him she was gone. I hurt for both of us; there is just not enough time with those we love.

Finally, after four years, Larry and our divorce case got to court. In the court room imagine my surprise when Larry's lawyer projected on a sixty-inch screen Randall without a shirt and stuck on the mirror blown up like a post card behind him was a business card saying Howard Johnson Inn also the date on the film was one day earlier than I said I arrived back in town. The icing on the cake, my military hat was on the rack above Randall in the picture, in plain view. Seems I laid the camera down when I got home and Larry stole the film. I never missed it, never thought about it. There were all kinds of guys with shirts off and shirts on people I went to basic with, but no matter if the picture was harmless or not it all looked bad especially after the Randall one. Well, the judge granted Larry a divorce although as an afterthought the judge said you know your marriage was technically not legal because you, looking at me, failed to wait thirty days after your last divorce was final to marry. What? All this for nothing. Oh well, twelve years too late with that information. The case was granted against me and most things awarded to Larry. I was allowed to live in the house until my youngest child was eighteen then Larry regained the property and I would have to move. Larry was to pay the mortgage since it was purchased with his GI Bill. I was awarded only $179 a month in child support total for all three children combined, which Larry vowed he would never pay by going to jail first. And he was true to his word. I never received one dime child support. To his credit he did give me his check book, fancy that, and if the kids needed anything I wrote a check for it and told him. This worked out. He took care of the kids not me. This was fine. Larry and I remained friends with benefits for years. After marriage we still never agreed on much but we both loved the kids and agreed on that. He has always done anything I ask him to do for the kids including fixing things at the house, watching the children, buying groceries if I needed them. He and a couple of my ex-boyfriends as well as my current boyfriend helped me get the cake, transport food, wash cars, etc. preparing for the wedding when my oldest daughter got married. After the wedding my pastor wanted to know where were all these helping exes were sleeping. I said where they always slept. He seemed stunned. I think he was expecting a more benign answer. I never made it better and laughed to myself. I get along with my oldest daughter's dad and all my ex-boyfriends even Larry, so all of them attended the wedding and all went home to their own beds. I might add all except my daughter's dad sat on the front row beside one another during the wedding. Larry said he was hanging around just to see the fight break out between the current boyfriend and the exes. He and I did better apart.

We could exchange glances, offbeat comments and laugh. Larry always had a dry sense of humor. In fact, some years later we spent a pleasant day and evening together at his apartment rehashing old times. It just happens to be the morning and afternoon of the day before he got married to someone else. I helped him choose his wedding attire. He prepared me breakfast and dinner and we made love all day. I thought he needed to feel what he would miss. You could say I was his bachelor party. Larry didn't care much about sex, but sometimes, just sometimes on very, very rare occasion he surprised me. This was one of his good days.

I responded to a column in a popular magazine about how there seemed to be a shortage of good men to date in Nashville. I wrote back and related the experiences I had with the local men. Using no names, I described their behavior. The liar who wouldn't know the truth if he fell on it. He had me in his vacationing, eight-year, live-in girlfriend's bed. He assured me the clothes I saw in the bathroom were his brother's girlfriend's clothes. The cheat was out with me while his women was in labor in the hospital having his baby. Found out about that from his sister who thought I knew. The sociopath who always claimed I was too good for him all the while I was a substitute for a smart ex-wife who got out in time. I later discovered his interest in me was I looked like his ex-wife except for her green eye color. I also found out when I left his apartment another woman would show up. He had rotating marathon women. Found this out because I forgot something one evening and came back two hours later to get it and he would not open the door. Almost burnt his apartment down that night. Thought about it, then decided he was not worth my time let alone jail time. On the TV, weather announcer who failed to tell me he was married till on a fishing trip his wedding ring appeared in his tackle box. Less I forget the Radio DJ who began to brag how he beat up his girlfriend who he thought was cheating on him. That was after he had been on a date with me. She couldn't date others but he could? Less I forget the singer who just happened to live with his female vocal partner, a living arrangement he carefully left out when telling me about himself. When I discovered that tidbit I checked the carpet between the bedrooms to see how bad the wear and tear was from foot traffic bedroom to bedroom. Found no damage because they probably were sleeping in the same room and bed. I had to agree the hassle of dating was overwhelming in Tennessee. No wonder the young do it they have more stamina.

One evening out of the blue I got a phone call from a man's voice saying, "I read what you said about me."

I said, "How did you know it was about you?"

He said, "I'm the singer."

I said, "Oh."

He asked if I'd like to go to a concert with him. I said, "Whose paying?"

He said, "Me, of course."

I said, "Just wanted to be sure these days you never know men think women will take care of them."

He said, "I can take care of myself, yes or no?"

I said, "Yes, where is your singing partner?"

He said, "That is what she is a partner, not a lover, and she is gone."

We talked every day until the concert. We went to the concert and had a great time. That was the beginning. All my other dating stopped. Thee guy whose apartment I wanted to burn down returned and wanted us to try again. It was too late. My trust meter for him was on zero. Johnnie was my permanent date. He was a great date, different. He loved to cook, go to movies, he was fun. He danced, he didn't care if I was late getting somewhere, he loved to shop as much or more than me. He'd drag me to all kinds of thrift shops, antique shops, even used car lots. The man was a shopping freak.

I had a party for a few friends on evening and Johnnie made barbecue. My guest loved it. One lady said you should open a restaurant. This is so good. The meat is hot and so tender, it's not dry and even the bones are hot. At the time he drove a cab and sang. Later he got into an accident and totaled the cab. He was so upset about it but coped well. Since he was doing nothing else during the day I talked him into opening a barbecue restaurant. We found a small store. It needed fixing up, but Johnnie said it's okay. He was there every day hammering and adding a new ceiling. I was surprised he did a great job. We filled out papers and begged for a small business loan to help with expenses. We never got the loan. We opened anyway with rented equipment and a very limited supply of meat. After the first half of the day we were out of meat but we had money. I quickly jumped in the car and made a run to the meat packing company to buy more. It was working. His sauce was unique, hot and delicious. Johnnie's sauce was so good people wanted to just buy it. I saw a guy just drinking it. Johnnie took pride in the preparation of every recipe. The meat was cooked well and held the flavor all the way through. He got up early each morning to start the fires, so the meat would slowly ready for the afternoon opening and we both stayed late to clean up. Business was good.

I gave up my daycare business to help him. Never regretted it. I looked forward to everyday being around him. We had fun, playing while working together. I couldn't be near him and not touch, lay my head on his back or hug him. We had this room size meat freezer in the back of the restaurant. It didn't work, it never got cold. We used it like an office. In the middle of the day or in the afternoon and late at night before he left to go sing, we made love in that freezer on the desk, on the floor over the chair it didn't matter it was so often we had to put a bell on the drive up window to hear the customers. Johnnie called it our midday tune up. He was fun to love. We worked hard every day except Sunday. We were up early and went to bed late. So just to get away we went on vacation with another couple on a cruise to Nassau in the Bahamas. We drove to Florida none of us had much money, so we ate in drive throughout picnic style. One morning early just before we got to the ship we stopped to bath and change. My girlfriend and I went into a service station bathroom. I crawled into the sink to washed as much of me as possible and changed clothes. My girlfriend just threw water all over herself like a shower. We left the guys at the car wash across the parking lot. When we returned Johnnie was naked wrapped in a poncho and had turned the wand you wash cars with on himself and there he stood showering in the car wash. Soaping up spraying water under the poncho and singing. We were laughing so hard we didn't see this lady trying to turn in to wash her car. She saw Johnnie though wrapped in that parka, guess she thought we were vagrants. I think she failed to see the humor because she quickly left. We quickly left, too, figuring she was going to call the police. At least we were all sparkly clean. Of course we bathed and changed again once on board the ship. That was a memorable time. I remember Johnnie saying they all looks better dressed then us. He said they'll see just wait till we unpack. We were all clothes horses and we had clothes. Our friends were as nutty as we were.

The cruise was wonderful beginning to end. There was so much to see and enjoy. Best of all having Johnnie, the man I adored, with me made everything perfect. It was a magical time. I will never forget it. Nothing I will ever do will trump that time. For thirteen years Johnnie had asked me to marry him the first time then each and every time I saw him. I always said no. His life style was a little rugged for me, but it didn't stop my fascination with him nor the love I developed for him. Marriage well that was a whole other animal. I had no Idea that the friendship we had would bloom into a comfort zone. He was easy to talk to, gentle and so sweet I just felt safe in his presence. He laughed more than he frowned and never took himself serious. If you said anything about me he felt would hurt my feelings he would quickly defend me. If I was out of his sight somehow I'd look up and from a distance even if he was on stage singing he would show me his teeth, nod and smile. He always thought he had to protect me. He was six feet, three inches, 315 pounds and I was four feet, eleven inches, 113 pounds. Even if other guys flirted with me he never interfered if they were respectful. Sometimes guys would send me drinks when I was alone at the bar or at a table. I didn't drink, so when Johnnie came to check on me he would drink the drinks. Even if I were out with friends and drinks suddenly appeared I'd let them sit cause sooner or later Johnnie would make his way to wherever I was like a magnet to say hi, drink the drinks, order me a coke and leave. I could count on him showing up at least once that night if I were out no matter where. I asked him once don't you get jealous when guys send me drinks or look at me or smile. He said no, men need to enjoy beauty long as it doesn't bother you. I'm just grateful you allow me to be the one you leave with. I'd drink your dirty bath water. I hope I die before you. I don't want to live here without you. Yeah, we had a mutual admiration society. I could sit and just listen to his voice talking or singing. When he entered the room and said good morning just that made me smile. His voice was velvet with a slight raspy sound. He sounded so much like Teddy Pendergrass singing that unless you really were good you could not tell their voices apart. I could, Johnnie's voice was silkier. He never wore his wedding band, so he appeared single. Women were all over him, on his lap taking pictures and just wild sometimes. Johnnie had a routine at the end of his performance he would pull the scarf from his jacket pocket wipe the sweat from his forehead and toss it into the audience. The women loved it but this act got expensive buying new scarfs all the time. I always coordinated and laid Johnnies clothes out for him for that night's appearance. One night I was out of little red scarves, so now what to do. Stores closed and he needed a scarf for the finale. Well, I reached down and took off my red bikini panties folded them nicely and put them in his pocket. Problem solved.

He came home that night, woke me up, and said, "Red, what did you put in my pocket?"

I said, "Well, we were out of scarves, so I put my panties in your pocket; they looked like a scarf. They were silky and red."

He said, "And you wore them very recently."

I said, "Yeah, how did you know?"

He said, "I pulled them out of my pocket, rubbed them across my face to mop the sweat, and I smelled you."

I said, "Oh! You mad?"

He broke into a smile and then a big laugh and said, "They loved it! Panties flying through the air just the kick the act needed; it was great! Do it again."

So now I got to wear the scarves they served a dual purpose. Johnnie was such a sport. I really had to work at it to make him mad. I always felt good when women went nuts over Johnnie. The more the women in the audience liked him the more the money. I understood their motivation and Johnnie's part in it. Jealous no not at all, I wanted him to succeed in his craft. It was hard not to go nuts listening to him sing those drippy love songs, watching him and not feel something. He put so much feeling into a song. Those big brown eyes, those long black eyelashes and pretty teeth, he was my teddy bear. I was aware I only shared his life and his talent. I didn't own it. I went nuts over him, too, every day, but I never threw my draws on stage at him like they did. For sure when I felt the need to throw my underwear at him I was always in them. I knew when Johnnie got done flirting, singing, hugging, and photo taking he would be home promptly. He would go in his pocket put all his money and the phone numbers he collected that night on the edge of the dresser, he'd say, "Red, these women will call tomorrow about 8:00 A.M."

I'd say, "Did you give them our number?"

He'd say, "Yeah. I was too tired to lie. That's the only number I know."

Consistently I'd say, "Did you tell them you were married?"

He'd say, "No, that's your job. I want them to keep coming back to hear me tomorrow, don't you? I'm an entertainer, that's what I do."

It took me awhile, but I began to understand. He played the game of single singer on stage. It was an act. Off stage when the music stopped the entertainer stopped and he became my husband. We took care of one another's needs, we applauded each other's successes, and boosted each other's ambitions. We never fought. Once he said I'm leaving for a while because if you were two feet taller I'd pound you on the head. I jumped on a stool and said if you were a foot shorter I'd pound you back. That was it he left. He returned later with a Hershey bar which we shared mouth to mouth. We did not argue We had a unique way to get our point across. Every time one of us did anything that annoyed the other we wrote it down on a list and attached a bothered me dollar amount to it. On New Year's Eve, we pulled out the list cuddled up with a glass of Asti Spumoni and read to the other their infractions collected the penalty fee, no checks allowed, for the offense. At the end of our list we usually had enough money from each other for a new coat or shoes. During the coming year we were careful not to leave the toilet seat up or bring the car home on empty again because the price doubled for a second offense. That night the list was torn. We toasted the new year, drank our champagne and never spoke of those infractions again.

My friends who were out and about would see Johnnie with some women on his lap taking pictures. They would get around to telling me they saw him. I'd say how many women were on his lap? they may say one. I'd say big as he is there should have been at least two more. We get more money per person per picture. He made no bones about his love for me. Unintentionally I heard one of Johnnie's friends trying to get him to double date with him and some women he talked with the night before. Johnnie said no. Red's all I need. I flirt and go on with those women when I work, but I'm off, I'm home being interested in anyone but Red is only what I do at work. I trusted Johnnie. After his performance, which usually ended late, tired he would come home sometimes eat, undress and shower the night away then come snuggle around my body hug me tight like a pillow and we would sleep. Some nights after Johnnie had fallen asleep I would wiggle loose from his bear hug grip, sit up in bed and pet his hair for hours watching him sleep. I use to think I've known this man thirteen years before we married. He asked me to marry him the minute we met and every time he saw me. I always said no. I wasted so much time. I didn't realize it could be so much fun married. Johnnie had a great sense of humor. He was so witty and so sweet and I could tell he got absolute joy from doing things to make me happy. Johnnie was my fifth husband. My Big Chocolate, good man.

The path to the inner peace I feel now and then as I watched Johnnie sleep was one I would not recommend. Nor would, given the opportunity, willfully have chosen for myself. The good and bad of my life to this point all worked out.

These events combined to enhance my growing process. Unfortunately, my growing process was not in a healthy garden. Growing in and through ashes, escaping the bugs was scary, often painful and inarguable dangerous. The happy/sad times and lonely days where many yet even with all the ordeals I do believe it took that and more to get me where I am. I learned. It was impossible not to learn. I still do not trust. I know my worth. I will not be used. I am not fragile, codependent, or naive. I know when love from anyone is one sided. I know how I will allow myself to be treated. I know what treatment I expect from others and the treatment I will not except. Open the sky, let it rain I will just grow stronger. I am resilient. The search is over.

CPSIA information can be obtained
at www.ICGtesting.com
Printed in the USA
LVHW081504150819
627772LV00029B/585/P